# eye of a hurricane

## STORIES BY
## RUTHANN ROBSON

Firebrand
Books
Ithaca, New York

The author wishes to acknowledge an Individual Artist's Fellowship from the State of Florida.

Several of the stories in this collection have appeared previously in the following periodicals: *Calyx, Catalyst, The Cimarron Review, Clinton St. Quarterly, Common Lives/Lesbian Lives, Conditions, Fireweed, Sagewoman,* and *Sojourner.*

Book and cover design by Betsy Bayley
Typesetting by Bets Ltd.

Printed on acid-free paper in the United States by McNaughton & Gunn

Library of Congress Cataloging-in-Publication Data

Robson, Ruthann, 1956-
    Eye of a hurricane : short stories / by Ruthann Robson.
       p.    cm.
    ISBN 0-932379-65-6 (alk. paper). — ISBN 0-932379-64-8 (pbk. : alk paper)
       1. Women—Fiction.    I. Title.
PS3568.03187E94    1989
813'.54—dc20                       89-23603
                                      CIP

# CONTENTS

# LEARNING
# TO
# SEE

The photograph is of a shoeless Mexican boy, about eight or nine, standing on a vacant, flat South Florida road. He and his surroundings are in gray tones. The single color in the photograph is the large, round orange the boy holds in front of him, as if offering it to the viewer. Orange. The fruit looks as if it is about to ripen and burst from the heat, as if it is about to send bright boiled juices down the boy's gray arm, down his gray ragged shorts to coagulate into a radiant orange puddle on the gray rocks of the sand.

She sells the photograph for $500, which she invests in more equipment for her darkroom. And what does the boy get? She tries not to ask herself that. She knows what he gets: years of picking oranges, moving north to pick strawberries and watermelons and maybe even farther north to pick apples. The couple who buy the print get another conversation piece for their Key Biscayne home.

The headaches are casual at first. Subtle. They come swathed in the white cloth of excuses: too much close work, the fumes of the fixer, the constant weight of two cameras around her neck, approaching deadlines.

She should go to a doctor, she knows. But there is always something else to do, some stupid last-minute assignment about a derailed train on Route 301. "Couldn't get anyone else, Kit. Could you please help us out?" And she always goes. She locks up the small apartment near the Gulf of Mexico and she goes. This is what being a free-lance photographer means, she thinks, being ready to document someone else's misfortune on a moment's notice.

Of course there is what other people call spare time, as in the question, "What do you do in your spare time?" For Kittrich, the small hours carved from the carcass of commitments are anything but spare. When she isn't on assignment or doing up a job, she is working. Real work. Her work. The thing in life she values most.

Kittrich stands for hours in her darkroom, with the equipment the Mexican boy's bewildered image had bought, and works. Harder and harder. She is exhibiting fairly steadily, being published in small art journals, and even consigning some work to a gallery or two. She is enjoying what people call moderate success, but she wants more. She wants never to be forced to take a photograph of a train wreck. So she squints away the headaches. She goes into the cruel fluorescent lights of the kitchen to eat colorless cereal because she is dizzy and thinks food might help. She continues to work.

Kittrich measures her life from the first time she looked through a viewfinder. "Photography is my life," Kittrich has said more than once: during an interview given to her alumni arts newsletter; when rejecting a proposal to live together; and several times in conversation with her mother.

In the interview she said she could still recall the first time she focused a camera, could distinctly remember thinking that the camera expanded rather than narrowed her vision.

In the interview she did not say she remembers how that initial click of the shutter sent an orgasmic shiver through her small body. In the interview she did not say that no sensation ever equalled that one, not even sex with Hank.

When she faints on assignment, months after the headaches had started, she decides it is time to see her doctor. Kittrich's fall had resulted in the cracking of a $200 lens. This is getting serious, she thinks; it is interfering with my work.

Her doctor pleads ignorance and refers her to a specialist connected with the University of Florida. He makes an appointment for her with the specialist, Dr. Safire, for next Friday at 1:00 p.m.

She wonders if Dr. Safire has blue-green eyes. She pictures him in black and white, except for the eyes.

On the Friday of her appointment, she loads her two cameras in the front seat of her car, more from force of habit than from expectation that she will see anything worth shooting on the way to Gainesville. "A good photographer takes his camera wherever he goes," one of her professors had told Kittrich. He needn't have. Her Nikon was her third eye. Her first eye.

Her first photograph was taken at the age of seven from the window of a moving DeSoto. The Tennessee mountains were perfectly focused and the tones of the gray rocks and gray trees and the guardrail could be easily distinguished. Even though her mother had yelled at her when she snapped the picture, her mother put the print proudly in the family album.

Years later, Kittrich used the snapshot in her first exhibition, a high school collection of black-and-white photographs she entitled "Learning to See." A judge remarked that Kittrich's photographs did justice to the textures of the mountains. Kittrich was ecstatic, and *texture* became her favorite word. When her family moved south, to a mostly below-sea-level peninsula called Florida, Kittrich had to learn to see the textures in things other than mountains.

She drives through the middle of the state toward the University, through the uneven land that had the audacity to aspire to hilliness. It has been a cold winter, and the late-ripening oranges still cling to the neat rows of trees in the groves. Pretty country. Mathematically fenced plots boast alfalfa and racehorses. Kittrich would like to live here someday, but she never takes photographs here. It is too serene, too much like Sunnybrook Farm. This is not the universe that Kittrich feels compelled to tell everyone about.

She did not always like what she was learning to see. At first she considered this a problem, but she capitalized on it until it became her trademark. By the time she got to college, she was devoted to photographing what she called social realities. While the other women in Kittrich's class made pleasant prints of pets and flowers, and while the men shot nudes—by which they meant naked women—Kittrich was developing negatives of garbage dumps, smokestacks, and dead animals.

"Photography as an art form reeks of death," she once said in class. "Even the film is made from the bones of animals." After that, no one bothered with Kittrich very much. Except Hank.

Just north of where she had photographed the train wreck several weeks ago, in what could pass for a small town, she sees *it*. She switches to the fast lane, crosses a dirt break in the grassy median and doubles back, driving slowly. When she sees *it* again, she pulls to the side of the road.

*It*. The perfect photograph. Kittrich could not have staged the scene better herself, even if she believed in posing photographs.

"They'll make a technician of you up there," Hank warned. But Kittrich went to the Rochester Institute of Technology against everyone's advice. Kittrich was not afraid of technique or of anyone making her into anything. She was rewarded at Rochester with a sweatless confidence inside the darkroom as well as outside.

She experimented with combining black and white with color. It was hardly an original idea. The old portrait photographs often possessed those blushed cheeks courtesy of a photographer's paintbrush. But Kittrich worked exclusively with photographs. She took color photographs and then black-and-white photographs of the color photographs, and so on. She played with isolating color, not for the sake of color, but always to make a point.

Any paint that had once graced the small frame house had peeled away long ago. Pieces of crumbled cinder block serve as a foundation separating the shack from the dusty ground. A Black male teenager stands on the porch, smoking a cigarette. To the left of the building sits an old black hearse, '62 maybe, with all its windows smashed. To the right blooms a brilliantly garish fuchsia azalea, at least fifty yards from other vegetation and as tall as a privacy hedge.

A prize-winning photograph waiting to be captured. Kittrich is already thinking of titles, exhibiting it, selling prints, and graciously accepting compliments.

She never allowed Hank to take photographs of her. Hank wanted to dress her in pastels and take her to a field and shoot rolls of Kodacolor film with her striking different poses. She refused. When Hank told her that she should be a sport, that although she was not beautiful, she was photogenic, she did not change her mind and she did not say thank you.

Why does her head spin so? Why doesn't her hand reach for either of the cameras? Why isn't she tripping the shutter and bracketing her exposures for insurance?

Damn. The young man's face is starting to change, his expression is going soft. The sun is shifting to cast the shadow of the house onto the azalea. Kittrich can feel the decisive moment slipping away like sweat down her back.

Hank sent her a photograph of a woman posed on a rock near a stream. The woman was wearing a white petticoat and camisole. If Kittrich felt anything, it was that the woman's skin tone looked a bit jaundiced against all that green foliage. It was winter in Rochester, and green was an especially hard color to imagine. Almost as hard as Hank metering the sharp Florida light.

Kittrich wrote Hank a critique of the technical aspects of the photograph. Then she went back to spend many hours in the darkroom facilities at the Rochester Institute. *Hibernation* replaced *texture* as her favorite word.

The dark-skinned teenager looks back at Kittrich, wondering what she is doing pulled to the side of the road and just sitting there staring. Kittrich sees what she has trained herself not to see: that her subject is more than a subject; that he is curious about her; that he might wonder for days why some white woman stopped and pointed her camera at him; that he might feel ashamed or mocked or even angry; that he might *feel*. As the teenager starts to come off the porch toward her, Kittrich shifts the car into gear and lurches up the grade onto the highway. One of the cameras rolls from the seat.

A few miles up the road, Kittrich swings into a Gateway discount gas station. She feels lightheaded and wants a Pepsi. When she looks at the faces of the people in the store, she sees only the face of the teenager on the porch steps. She thinks she can hear him: *What will you give me if you take my photograph? Nothing! You will sell it to pay the rent on your fancy beach house. I make your photograph and you give me nothing in return. How do we know that the Indians weren't right? That you aren't stealing my soul?*

"Must everything you do make some kind of social statement? This can be very tedious." Or so one professor at the Rochester Institute wrote on the evaluation of her "Techniques in Black and White" portfolio. The professor had a highly respected, if somewhat limited, reputation based on his highly detailed photographs of precious gems. Kittrich discarded the evaluation, keeping only the *A.*

She protests to the Black teenager in her mind that her house is far from fancy, though maybe a bit overpriced, and it isn't even on the beach. Stupid, she thinks; besides, that is not the point. She defends herself by saying that she wants to change social conditions, that by photographing him she is letting his expression articulate all the things he really wants to say. Yet she knows she has no idea what he really wants to say. Her mind pastes the word *exploit* on his lips.

Even at the office of the specialist, when she should be concentrating on other things, Kittrich cannot evict the teenager from her cloudy mind. Dr. Safire seems as if he is on the other side of a FOG #5 lens filter. She isolates words from the doctor's mouth, words like *hospital, tests, afternoon,* words like brightly colored balls in an otherwise gray vocabulary. Dr. Safire is deep brown, like the Mexican boy. She sees the boy as a photograph, eternally holding that bright orange. That boy is probably a teenager by now, she thinks.

In the hospital, the nurses are all friendly and call her Kitty, as if they are maiden aunts who have known her all her life, as if she is a small cute animal that will soon be a nuisance. In a spunkier mood, she would have taken shots at them, patronizingly calling them by diminutives, attempting to be an equal. But there is never equality between the sick and the healthy.

Dr. Safire, in his green smock, comes to speak with her. She is surprised to see him in the hospital. "CAT-scan," he says, "like taking a picture of your brain."

"You should understand that," he smiles. She does not remember telling him her profession.

When she came back to Florida from the Rochester Institute, she naturally slid into being a free-lancer for several newspapers, some underground publications, an environmental group, and whoever needed her peculiar talent of rendering reality as a black-and-white problem to be solved.

She also pursued her style of making social statements into social art. She thought the photograph of the Mexican boy with the orange was a watershed of her efforts. Yet she sometimes wondered whether the stylish couple who bought the expensive print saw the photograph the same way she did.

Later, back in the office, the specialist is not smiling. He is preparing me, she thinks. For the worst.

She looks at him hard and suddenly wants to touch him, the way she hasn't wanted to touch anyone in years. Now it isn't enough to see texture, she wants to feel it. Kittrich notices with a shock that she is not previsualizing the doctor, not imagining him as a photograph of himself. It seems unnatural.

She does not want to photograph him.

She wants to know him.

"No one knows what causes these things. Yours has been in rapid growth for some time and is pressing against the optic nerve. My opinion is that it is presently inoperable, but we want to consult another doctor, of course. Here, let me show you the CAT-scan results."

To Kittrich, the tumor looks like a blot on a negative, a piece of dust that can be brushed away, a splash of chemical to be compensated. It looks unreal, insignificant. Photographs make everything look that way, she thinks.

As insignificant as Hank's wedding, although her mother had not seen it that way. "I've never heard of such a thing in all my born days," her mother had sighed. Despite her mother's shaking head, Kittrich had packed her car and headed to Miami to take photographs of

Hank's wedding. After all, Kittrich reasoned, I am the best photographer Hank knows.

After leaving Dr. Safire's office, a list of possible sources for second opinions in hand, Kittrich tries to remember the color of the specialist's eyes. They escape her. But two of his words hold her tight: *blindness* and *death*. Words he did not use. Words he was careful to avoid. Words he will later use when describing this sad case to his wife. Kittrich knows.

Death. How clichéd.

Almost required if she is ever to cross that nebulous border between good and great. She pans her liberal arts education for artists who died young, who were "cut down in their prime." Let's see: Keats and Isadora Duncan and Flannery O'Connor and even George Eastman, founder of Kodak. Eastman was a suicide though. She wasn't sure whether that should count.

Even the blindness is a cliché. Who could forget Bette Davis in *Dark Victory?*

"A photographer's eye is his everything," Hank said. He was explaining why male photographers often slept with their female models.

"If his eye is his everything, then why does he bother to employ certain other parts of his body so steadily?" Kittrich looked squarely in Hank's gray eyes.

"You have no aesthetic sense," he laughed. Kittrich continued watching an old movie on television.

My eye has never been my everything, Kittrich thinks while driving home. Never. It's my mind that takes the picture. My aesthetic sense is in my mind, in my conscience. And I still have that.

For a while.

Kittrich thinks again of the Mexican boy holding the orange, forever healthy in a rich person's foyer. He will survive me.

Kittrich thinks again of the Black teenager near the hearse, forever wondering why she stopped. He will die with me, or soon after. Both of us casualties of society's failures, political and medical. Inoperable.

Back in her apartment a few blocks from the placid Gulf of Mexico, Kittrich thinks that maybe she should call Hank and arrange to have dinner. She's heard he's back in town, possibly divorced. Or maybe she should send him a photograph he had wanted that she had been saving for an exhibit. There's no reason not to be generous now.

Instead, she sets the more expensive of the two Nikons on a tripod and attaches a six-foot-long cable release cord. She moves in front of the lens and presses the button which trips the shutter. She has become her own social statement.

"The only thing I've ever known is when to trip the shutter, an intuitive grasp of the decisive moment, the moment when everything that needs to be seen is showing itself in the right light."

Kittrich had written that down in the notebook she kept in her camera bag. She wanted to say it to the woman who interviewed her for the alumni arts newsletter. She wanted to say it to Hank when he criticized her for her lack of social grace. She wanted to say it to somebody, someday.

Kittrich thinks she has lost even her intuition, lost it this morning near the Black teenager and the hearse and the shack being mocked by that pompous flowering bush. The vision she has struggled for years to perfect has popped from her eyes as easily as dried contact lenses, evaporated the moment she could not reach for the camera. She was deprived of insight by the dark eyes of a teenager who looked back at her with curiosity.

She starts to cry.

"I'll look for the Mexican boy. I'll find him. Give him a print. Give him the five hundred dollars. Plus interest." The words come out of Kittrich's mouth like soap bubbles with tiny rainbows.

Kittrich wants to know if the Mexican boy looked back at her too, and she hadn't noticed. She wants to bargain for a few minutes of the boy's life, even a life picking oranges before they are sprayed with color.

"Anything. I'd give anything."

The only thing Kittrich has to trade is photographs.

The photograph is of a barefoot white woman, youngish, standing in front of a vacant white wall. There is such a high contrast between the whites and black of her dress that there appears to be no gray. The only other color in the photograph is the red of a large, sparkling pin. It is stuck in the curve of her breast, as if she is hiding it from the viewer, as if it is real. Ruby real. The gaudy piece of costume jewelry looks as if it is about to explode and burrow into the woman's flesh, as if it is about to summon up crimson fluid down the woman's black dress, down her white legs, to curdle in an erratic scarlet pool on the bleached sheepskin of the rug.

She will never sell this photograph.

# GROWING AVOCADOS

Four blue toothpicks have been stabbed into each pit, so that every sea-urchined creature is partially submerged in water and partially suspended above the rim of the glass. The ledge above the kitchen sink is a mob of attempted rootings, not all of them successful. On the other side of the window, a fuchsia blossom bangs against the shadows of the afternoon sun. Deeper in the yard, near a single-storied structure, a discarded avocado pit which had rotted in water now pushes a bruised root through the soil.

Two women live in the house, on the land. Each woman has proudly wondered aloud whether a casual observer would know this is a women's house, women's land. Each woman has worried silently whether the house or land can share other secrets. The women dream with their heads tilted toward each other. They dream that their secret grows as wild and as obvious as the potted avocado plant on the wicker chest beneath the blinds of their narrow bedroom window. The women are afraid their secret will come to light and the women are afraid that it won't. They are afraid. They are afraid of each other.

Charleen is a teacher. Philosophy. At Three Rivers Junior College, she is the only person who teaches the subject. Other teachers, who like to be called professors as much as Charleen does, debate whether or not there should be any curriculum offerings in philosophy. The junior college, which has been enrolling students for the past twelve years, holds Friday forums with topics such as, "Liberal Arts or Liberal Trades?" and "Are We *Under* Undergraduate Schools?" Charleen has been teaching at the school for less than an academic year, so she tries to attend these meetings.

Sometimes, like today, she chooses not to go. Charleen cannot bear to be seen by the other faculty members this afternoon. The book contract she was going to have fell through, and although she tries to feel smart because she did not share the possibility with any of her colleagues, Charleen cannot accept her consolation prize. A contract with the biggest textbook publisher would have meant a raise, an impeccable credential, a shot at a better job. Everyone would have envied her, would have whispered about something other than her personal life. Everyone would have realized that she was just as good— better—even though she graduated from a third-rate university and teaches an unrated subject. But now, nothing will change.

Charleen pushes past a budded bush, short-cutting her way to her $225 a month, 11% interest, Nissan station wagon. The spring sun heats the skin under her too-tight black slacks and tweedlike jacket. Her students have been promising her that spring will be gorgeous. Charleen discounts their assurances because they are mostly local kids who seem apologetic about the incessant rain and frosty nights. During an epistemology lecture, Charleen had used the awful weather as an analogy. She had told the students that the harsher the winter, the more pleasing spring seemed, regardless of spring's actual character. She had written the word *phenomenology* on the blackboard. She had explained to the class that it was like banging your head on the wall: the harder you banged, the better it felt when you stopped.

She drives the new but narrow road into the country. Blood-colored soil, netted by giant gouged roots, defines her way. When she arrives at her turn, to an older but also narrow road, she holds the wheel with one hand and twists out of her jacket.

Then she smiles. She knows she is almost home when she reaches this long, sloping-southward field of hay. She loves this hill because it refuses to be green or garish, despite the coaxings of the surrounding land. This rise reminds her of Deirdre's hair, of Deirdre's thighs.

Deirdre makes jewelry. Silver. She works all day in her one-story studio behind the thickly wooded hill, filling orders for the stores in South Florida that stock her creations. This late afternoon she feels a satisfaction with her progress that has recently become quite rare. She shines her planishing hammer and hangs it on the rack between the tack hammer and the chasing hammer. She straightens the anvils, the dapping block and punch, and the mandrels. She puts the tops on the pickle acid and the flux, checks that both tanks for the oxy-acetylene are off, and wipes the tripoli and rouge wheels of the buffer. She slips an earring in her pocket to show Charleen.

Deirdre's Nike AirSoles follow no particular path up the mossed hill, but wander under the dogwoods and past a plot of daffodils drowning in brown leaves. Deirdre cannot imagine herself as anything other than a visitor on her own land. She judges the sun too shallow to penetrate the web of trees and the air too damp to mark the first day of spring. She misses her house in Miami, forgetting for a moment the agony of daily life as a physician's wife, remembering only the hibiscus, the oleander, the swift scent of the ocean, walking and holding hands with Jana. It was true, as Charleen had said, that one could bang metal into bracelets anywhere. Still, Deirdre thinks she would be more regularly inspired if she did not feel so inappropriate in her cotton clothes.

Yet she smiles. She sees the crest of the cedar A-frame house, bordered with tangles of blooming bushes. She begins breaking the thin branches, borrowing beauty with the justification that it will fade anyway. There is an almost tropical pink, and a delicate pink, and a pink that seduces red. There is a small flower so tightly open it could be mistaken for a bud, and a florid mouth full of tongues. There are purples, whites, petals, pistils, yellows, and the sweetest tangerine-colored anthers.

Variety excites Deirdre. She spreads her bounty on the kitchen table, then fetches her sketchbook and charcoal pencil from upstairs. Perhaps a pair of earrings. Perhaps an amulet. Finished sketching, she hums textures to herself as she bends the branches into glasses of water. One glass for the coffee table. One glass for each bookcase.

A big glass on the bedroom chest next to her favorite avocado, nearly three-feet high. One glass—of madder yellow flowers, she laughs to herself—for the bathroom. On the white birch kitchen table, she places the most disarmingly pink blossoms in a small vase she brought back from that long-ago honeymoon in Japan. She stuffs an oversize goblet with all the remnants, jamming it onto the windowsill amid her variously rotting and sprouting avocados.

The two women sit at their white birch table, in their house, on their land. In the gradual twilight, they look similar as half-sisters. They are both white, with overgrown eyebrows and slim fingers. Their hair is brown, darker on the legs than on the head. Their backs are straight and their irises more blue than not. They both have jutting bicuspids. One of the women is taller by three inches, bigger boned, softer spoken, and has a scar on her left cheek. And one on her ankle and one on her forehead. And a mending wrist.

The women quietly eat the black beans and rice Deirdre has simmered. They chew without comment. There are no complaints and no compliments.

"It's amazing all the different flowers that grow up here," Deirdre says, adding, "by the house, I mean. I mean, up here, by the house."

"What different flowers are you talking about?" Charleen asks.

"The ones outside. By the house. I mean, I brought them inside. I thought you'd like them. Do you like them? I thought they were a nice mixture. All so different."

"They're all the same," Charleen says.

"They are all the same," Charleen says again.

"They're all rhododendrons, stupid. I thought you'd learn something like that in one of those garden clubs doctors' wives belong to."

"I thought those pink ones were azaleas." Deirdre gestures to the Japanese vase on the table.

"An azalea *is* a rhododendron, stupid."

The women look at each other. A trace of amusement, of victorious retreat, glimmers in Charleen's eyes.

"Lovers shouldn't argue about botany," Charleen says, reaching across the table to smooth Deirdre's tense shoulders.

Deirdre nods.

"Are the beans too mushy?" Deirdre risks a question after a few minutes.

"Findhorn phoned today," Charleen answers.

"Oh, what did he say?

"Only that the whole deal is off. Only that the marketing people don't want someone like me. He was very apologetic, of course. He apologized if he'd led me on or anything. He said he was sure it would go through." Charleen twirls the Japanese vase between her slim fingers. "But the marketing people, the marketing people think it would be better if the author has either graduated from a top-flight university or teaches at a university rather than a junior college. They need to sell the book. They can't market someone like me."

"I'm sorry."

"What are you sorry for? You didn't do it, did you? It's not your fault."

"I mean, I'm sorry. It's just an expression." Deirdre leans back in her chair, but not soon enough. Porcelain hits her on the jaw, Charleen's fingers still holding the neck of the vase. Water runs down Deirdre's throat. A petal falls on Deirdre's collar.

Deirdre stands and moves against the sink, facing the window. The smaller woman spins Deirdre around, slapping her and screaming.

"You and your stupid flowers."

The rhododendrons on the sill scatter to the floor.

"You and your goddamn slimy growths."

Glasses shatter.

"You think you're going to grow trees on the fucking windowsill."

A hurled avocado pit stabs Deirdre's shoulder.

"If you hate it here so much, why did you ever want to live up here?"

Toothpicks glaze an eye.

"You think you can buy anything with your doctor husband's money. Well, you can't buy me, you whoring cunt."

A fist in the stomach, on the thigh.

"You think you're not a dyke 'cause you were married. Let me tell you something. You're more queer than I'll ever be."

Charleen shoves Deirdre to the floor. A silver earring spills from Deirdre's pocket.

Charleen rips Deirdre's thin cotton shirt. Two unsunned breasts blink in the day's last light.

Charleen bites. And bites. Only when the kitchen lapses into total darkness do the bites become soft. Deirdre nibbles back, her mouth swelling.

Deirdre sits on the back step of her studio. The cold concrete is thick with pollen. She wishes there were a clearing, perhaps a pond, somewhere she could get a tan deep enough to cover. It is Saturday, the second day of spring, but a crackling drizzle descends, falling from the live oaks which habitually hold their leaves until the last possible moment. Deirdre wishes for Miami, for a Miami with Jana, for the Miami before Charleen arrived.

The violence had started there. Deirdre recalls how quick Charleen had been to blame the heat, to blame the aftertaste of Deirdre's divorce, to blame Deirdre's perplexed family or Deirdre's cautious friends. At the time, it had seemed logical to move away from the memories as well as from the urban crime. Rural North Florida seemed like the perfect place for Deirdre to transform her lump-sum alimony into acreage near the school where Charleen had an outstanding job offer. It had seemed possible that things would change.

Deirdre wants to heal herself, but she feels like she is in a universe of unfamiliar tools. All her past healings, and there have been many she reminds herself, have relied upon the ocean. When Jana had left to go back to Nicaragua, Deirdre had walked miles along the beach, becoming more and more malleable, until her soul opened to the horizon.

She knows she will get lost if she walks now: everything twists in the forest, and the obscured sun gives no direction. To walk in the woods, she thinks, requires a destination. She has nowhere to go. No friends or family here. No one. She longs for Jana, her best friend still, her best lover ever. Jana would know what to do.

Deirdre thinks that she could go and try to find a women's shelter or flag down a sheriff's car, but she wonders what would she tell them? *My lover—she beats me.*

And if the counselor or the officer asks what happened next, what can she say?

*My lover, she beats me. And then we make love. The same fingers that leave a bruise on my throat feel so fine when they stroke my neck. The same tongue that calls me cunt feels like a miracle when it goes there.*

Charleen wakes with shame. Again. She had promised herself that this would not happen again. She had promised Deirdre.

But it is difficult for Charleen not to blame Deirdre: Deirdre of the mythically easy life who has never struggled. Charleen thinks that Deirdre can never understand how painful it is to go out every day into a world that whispers dyke behind her back. Charleen is sorry, but believes that Deirdre should be sorrier.

Charleen walks through the house looking out windows, looking for Deirdre. She sees only those sinister rhododendron blossoms—hundreds of the same shade of pink—in the bedroom, on the kitchen floor, pressing against the windows. Charleen laughs that Deirdre had been naive enough to believe all those flowers were different. Charleen slips on the wet floor, swearing as her feet slide, finally regaining balance. Perhaps Deirdre had known, she thinks, and was only mocking. Yes, Charleen says almost aloud, Deirdre was like that: provoking her one minute and kissing her the next.

Charleen breathes. She will show her. If Deirdre thinks she's so smart, disappearing on this beautiful spring morning just perfect for a walk, disappearing without making coffee or cleaning up the mess she made the night before, she'll find out how stupid she really is.

Charleen hurriedly dresses. She pulls down Deirdre's largest leather suitcase from the attic crawlspace. She packs two of Deirdre's favorite pants and takes her most comfortable shoes. Charleen then stuffs into the suitcase as many of her own clothes as it will hold. She is forcing it closed on the bed when she brushes against the plant on the chest. She jerks the stem free from the dirt, shakes it on the rug, then jams the plant into the suitcase.

When the bulky suitcase is anchored on the Nissan's roof rack and lashed down with elastic ties, Charleen notices that there are long roots protruding. It takes her several tries before she can rip off the offending pieces. She drives away, reddish dirt on both of her hands.

# ARVA'S
# TRIANGLES

Arva packs two bags of fresh ice against the slant of Colleen's jawbone, making a bulky V under the chin. Pushing the grass-green comforter around Colleen's neck to keep the ice in place Arva arranges her own green-striped (and now blood-striped) pillow under Colleen's clipped sandy hair, then runs down the thirty-two hot steps into Mother Right Bookstore. Arva does this eleven times during the four hours of the afternoon before she locks the store half an hour early without closing out the register.

Colleen has been drifting around the bright light of consciousness. She has sensed Arva replacing the plastic bags of ice, has sensed Arva smoothing her forehead, patting her hands. Colleen knows that she and Arva have been exchanging marvelously profound thoughts, but she cannot tell whether these conversations occurred in that hazy realm outside her own mind.

In her bedroom, Arva slants the blinds to admit the shadows of twilight. Colleen opens her eyes and clutches for Arva. Arva sits on her bed and takes Colleen's hand.

The clasped hands are both white, both womanly. They share a similar strength with their squared nails, light calluses, and unpampered knuckles. One hand is more well-worn, darker but less tan, and has a series of partially hidden scars on both the back and the palm from a dog's incisors trying to kiss each other through childhood flesh. The other hand, Colleen's hand, slackens suddenly.

"There is a lot of pain," Colleen says. "Didn't Dr. Carr give you a shot for me? Can't you give it to me now?"

Arva smiles, a little surprised at Colleen's lucidity at remembering the needles of Demerol which now rest on a wicker shelf in the bathroom. The oral surgeon had asked Arva if she knew how to give an injection, and Arva had hesitated before she nodded vertically. The doctor had handed her two prepared needles along with a written prescription for Dilaudid. "Wisdom teeth aren't usually so serious," Dr. William Carr announced to Arva, "even impacted ones. But Colleen's teeth were terribly tough." The doctor, who had known Colleen all her life as he said twice, asked Arva if she would be able to take care of Colleen all afternoon. Arva remembered that part-time Leah would need to get to a class as soon as Arva returned to Mother Right, but she answered the doctor, "Yes."

The doctor had smiled then, with his perfect oral surgeon teeth. "Are you a classmate of Colleen's?" he asked, attempting to picture Arva as a returning student.

"No."

"Oh. Well, then do you work with her?"

"Actually, I'm her boss."

"Wow, not everyone can get their boss to pick them up from the doctor's." He laughed in that airy way men feign when they think they have discovered the something more that was not meant to meet their eyes.

Arva had neither joined in the doctor's laughter nor parted her lips to show her unperfected teeth.

"I have to pee," Colleen pronounces.

Arva helps Colleen to the small bathroom, balancing her on the toilet. She maneuvers Colleen onto the edge of the bathtub, adjusts the light, and rubs witch hazel on the muscle of Colleen's left arm. Arva stabs the needle once, not forcefully enough. A slant of blood forms. Arva's second aim is more professional, she pushes the plunger, pulls out the needle directly. She looks at Colleen's swollen jaw. She rests her head against the mint-green tiled wall.

"Shit," is all Arva can say.

They sit on the edge of the bathtub for long, long moments.

As the Demerol slips into Colleen's bloodstream, she wonders what is wrong with Arva. Colleen thinks that Arva cannot be squeamish about a mere needle. Colleen has never seen the older woman anything but competent, strong, and self-possessed. For the last year, Colleen has confided in Arva. Colleen took the part-time job at Mother Right only so that she would have guaranteed, even if subject to interruption, slots of time with Arva. Colleen needs to talk with Arva more than she needs the money, given her grandmother's promise to pay her tuition and living expenses while she goes to college. She likes to tell Arva about her lover, Goldie; to tell Arva things she could never tell Goldie. Colleen once told Arva that sometimes things did not feel quite solid until she told them to Arva. But now Colleen is floating, unable to talk, unable any longer to wonder what Arva could be thinking.

Arva is thinking of Theresa—of plunging needles into the arms, the thighs, the stomach of her first woman lover. Arva is feeling rushes from twenty years ago, when an unpleasant rush was better than no rush at all. Arva is seeing collapsed veins, blood spurting on rags tied around limbs. Arva is remembering Theresa's pale skin, her pale hair, her pale life and paler death.

"Shit," Arva says again, before guiding Colleen from the bathroom to the land between the green-striped sheets. Arva changes the ice packs, feeds Colleen two more pills, and then tries to spoon some asparagus soup into Colleen's numbed mouth. Colleen clamps shut against the soup.

Arva lights an amber candle and crawls into her apartment's only bed. It is less strange to be in bed with this young woman than Arva would have thought. Colleen grabs for Arva, as if by instinct. Arva's left hand is intertwined with both of Colleen's hands. Arva's right hand balances the book she is predictably reading: yet another thick treatise on the Holocaust flickers in the candle's thin flame as Arva searches for mentions of gypsies.

When Arva begins a passage about Nazi doctors implanting women with the sperm of apes, she decides she has had enough for one night. She closes the book, putting it on the low bookcase beside her bed, and blows out the candle. Her movements jostle Colleen, who tenses her body. Arva strokes Colleen's shoulders.

"How do you feel?" Arva whispers.

"Fine. O.K. Some pain."

"Rest."

"Talk to me."

"Do you want me to read to you?" Arva thinks that the Holocaust book will not be appropriate.

"No. I want you to talk to me. You never really talk to me. You give me advice and you tell me lots of neat things, but you never really talk to me." Colleen draws Arva's hand to her wet face. "I tell you everything, everything. You tell me about Lesbian literature or witchcraft in the Middle Ages or the paintings of Frida Kahlo. You never tell me about you."

Even while Arva decides it is the painkillers that are making Colleen cry, she realizes Colleen is right. Absurdly, Arva feels assaulted.

"Well, I never thought you were very interested." Arva's voice is low and defensive. Arva had, in fact, often judged Colleen self-centered in that seamlessly oblivious way that only an upper-class woman in her early twenties could be.

"I'm afraid to pry. I know you're a very private person."

"Oh." Arva smooths Colleen's hair.

"I mean, you know all about my crazy parents, my grandmother, my sex life with Goldie, all my professors, and all my former lovers. I don't even know where you were born."

"Ask me," Arva says. "You can ask me anything."

"Where were you born?"

Arva laughs in the dark, disarmed by Colleen's narcotic sweetness. "I was born in New York. During the War—and not the Viet Nam War." Arva lets another little laugh from her lips. "My mother escaped Old Europe with the black triangle still sewn to her shirt. She was a gypsy, marked for extermination. She was lucky enough to have some distant relations in Brooklyn. She was seventeen and six-months pregnant with me when she arrived. She went to work in a munitions factory. I was born in its bathroom."

"What about your father?

"What father?"

"You must have a father." Colleen is matter of fact.

"My father is a dash on my birth certificate. Maybe he was a Hitler Youth who raped my mother. Or maybe a man with authority to provide her passage. I never asked her. I never wanted to know. My mother was my father. She was enough. I never wanted to remind her about him. She was more than enough for me."

"Did you have a happy childhood?"

Arva restrains herself from being derisive. "Yes," she says simply.

"Did your mother know how to tell fortunes?"

Arva hates it when stereotypes are accurate, but does not think it reason enough to lie. "She did. After the War, when the good jobs for women were gone, she made some money that way. She also cut hair. I think she stole sometimes. Once we lived in a car and I think she had stolen it. It was a two-tone blue Hudson."

"Wow. How did you ever wind up here?" Colleen's voice is dreamy.

Arva assimilates the fact that she has wound up someplace. She thinks there are worse places to wind up than a small university town notable for being two hundred miles from anywhere else.

"I don't know," she answers hoarsely. "My mother died. I tried to support myself in the only ways I knew how. I told fortunes. I thieved. I cut hair. There was a war in Asia that made me afraid. I felt like the ghost of my mother. I got pregnant and nearly died from a gypsy abortion. I got tired of being poor and hungry. I fell in with some hippies who thought I was authentic, that my life was somehow really real and romantic. I followed a woman who was coming here. She drew me into the bookstore collective. When the collective split, I was the only one interested in staying, so I did. And I'm still here."

Arva expects another question, until she realizes Colleen is sleeping. She strokes Colleen's hair in the darkness, wondering why she just told this young woman—this girl—more about herself than she has told anyone in the last two decades.

It is certainly more than she has told either of her two long-standing lovers: Suzanne in Atlanta and Marita in Miami. It is a good portion of a day's drive to either of them, and Arva knows the distance is not merely geographic. Sometimes Arva stands in Mother Right Bookstore, near the burgeoning Women's Spirituality shelf, and angles her arms in front of her. She extends one arm to the north and one arm to the south, reaching with the fingers of her left hand for Suzanne's African ear, with the fingers of her right hand for Marita's scarved head. Sometimes either one or the other will visit her.

When Suzanne, the artist, stays in the apartment, Arva makes wild phone calls to Miami. When Marita, the travel agent, flies to stay in that same apartment, Arva books flights to Atlanta she will later cancel. Arva sleeps in her bed with either Suzanne or Marita, but she always sleeps restlessly. Arva makes tea and listens endlessly as Suzanne monologues about raising an adolescent named Summer. Arva lights candles and strokes smooth skin as Marita cries about her brother's fight against AIDS. Arva makes long love to each of the women. Arva holds them as they rage against the universe, as they try to understand the world, as they complain about their cities. Sometimes Arva lets them make love to her. But Arva never tells their fortunes and she never tells them her's.

Arva slips into sleep, until Colleen starts to retch. Blood and bile spatter the green carpeting as Arva pulls Colleen to the bathroom. Colleen crouches over the toilet. Colleen is having dry heaves. Finally, she needlessly flushes.

"You're all right." Arva stands in the bathroom doorway.

"Yes. My mouth hurts. I'm dizzy. Why am I vomiting? I hate to vomit. I need another shot."

"Not until you eat something. The painkillers are nauseating you. Get back in bed."

At 2:35 a.m., Arva is dishing out vanilla ice cream for Colleen. Arva watches Colleen to make sure she eats every spoonful. Then she gives her two more pills.

Colleen is crying again.

"I want another shot."

"Maybe later."

"I want Goldie," Colleen sobs.

Arva sits beside Colleen, refusing to comfort her. Arva allows herself to feel tangential in the unlit bedroom. Only when she thinks Colleen is asleep does Arva flatten her back against the bed.

"What do you think of Goldie?" Colleen asks, slurring the words into sleep.

"Nothing," Arva answers, as she has every time Colleen has asked this question.

"Tell me another story. Talk to me about your life."

"My life has many stories," Arva whispers, "like most lives."

"Tell me," Colleen breathes deeply. "Tell me about your first lover."

Arva is silent. It is the silence of a woman who can make a living selling books but remain deeply suspicious of language. It is the silence of avoiding a violation—of Theresa, of her love for Theresa, of herself—by packaging events as a bedtime story.

In the morning, after two more vomiting episodes by Colleen, Arva showers, dresses in jeans and a Witches Heal lavender T-shirt, and heads down the stairs to Mother Right Bookstore. She checks on Colleen throughout the morning in regular fifteen-minute intervals, whether or not there are customers in the store. At noon she makes Colleen eat cream of broccoli soup, and then expertly gives her the other needle of Demerol. She expects that this will let Colleen sleep through the evening, so she is surprised to find Colleen sitting at the kitchen table using the phone in the late afternoon. By the time Arva closes the store and counts out the register, Goldie Suarez is at the door.

"Hey." Goldie walks into the only woman's bookstore within two hundred miles for the second time in her life.

"Hello."

"Wow. I hear you've really been taking care of Colleen. You deserve a medal. I'm glad you're doing that. I'm awful at those things. She told me she's been puking. God, puke makes me sick. Though I guess if I would have known it was going to be so bad, I would have hung around."

"Why didn't you think it would be so bad?" Arva ices her eyes to look at the clear blue of Goldie's irises.

When two women perceive themselves as enemies rather than allies, neither woman sees beyond appearances. Arva sees a young woman with unevenly chopped blonde hair and black boots. Arva sees a bleached, torn shirt over khaki-green pants and an undecipherable tattoo on one arm. Arva sees a German woman who was born in Argentina. Arva sees a rich Americanized woman, a shallow woman.

Goldie sees an old dyke running a bookstore.

Arva leads Goldie into her apartment and then into her bedroom where Colleen is druggily dreaming. Goldie sits on the bed and reaches for Colleen. She kisses her chest.

Taking the stairs two or three at a time, Arva goes down the brown hallway into Mother Right Bookstore. She telephones Suzanne and then Marita. She talks to each of her lovers for more than an hour without ever mentioning the couple upstairs on her bed. Instead, Arva talks about giving and needing, about uneven relationships, about childless mothers. She talks in abstractions, but each of her lovers asks whether Arva is mad at her. Arva says no. This satisfies both Suzanne and Marita, and neither woman asks anything else.

Upstairs on the bed, Colleen and Goldie are not making love as Arva suspects, but are talking.

"Arva sure is a saint to take care of you. I'm sorry I can't be around, but I've got lots of loose ends to tie up."

"That's O.K.," Colleen answers honestly, thinking about their upcoming summer in Europe. Goldie is leaving for New York in the morning. They will meet in Paris next Monday.

"This room is a little creepy," Goldie says, shifting her weight on the bed.

"I don't think so." Even through the Dilaudid and remnants of Demerol, Colleen is defensive about Arva.

"Really? I guess it's just this dark wood furniture. And that mural of leafless trees over there, painted on that green wall. Do you think Arva painted that? Is it supposed to be the great outdoors or what? I've never seen that woman go outside."

"I like it. This room reminds me of a forest." Colleen is definite. "Besides Arva is a gypsy, you know."

"Oh." Goldie says, disliking the admiration thick in Colleen's comment. "I didn't think there were any gypsies left. Just watch out she doesn't give you the evil eye or something."

Colleen is sleeping again and does not hear Goldie's warning. Neither does she hear Goldie leaving or Arva returning to her bed.

Even after Colleen is coherent and the pain nearly gone, she continues to stay at Arva's apartment. Colleen works a few hours at Mother Right Bookstore, goes to her own house to get changes of clothes, buys a piece of leather luggage for her flight on Sunday. She always returns to Arva's apartment, as if she lives there.

Arva cannot understand why Colleen stays. Perhaps she just hates to be alone, Arva surmises without experiential comprehension of such a state. But even less can Arva understand why she allows Colleen to stay, why she wants her to stay. Perhaps because Colleen is leaving in less than a week, Arva thinks, trying to discount memories of her irritation at the second night of briefer visits by either Suzanne or

Marita.

Two women can quickly create a domestic pattern. Arva and Colleen sleep side by side, hugging. Colleen tells anecdotes. Sometimes she cries about her parents. Arva allows Colleen to ask her questions, and Arva answers them, except when Colleen questions Arva about Goldie. Arva decides Colleen is looking for confirmation that Goldie is vacant.

One night, when the phone rings very late, Arva answers it. She whispers and consoles the long-distance woman who is crying. Arva's voice is almost a chant. After a long time, she laughs low. She says, "I love you, too," before she hangs up.

When Arva returns to the bed, Colleen is stiff. Arva waits for Colleen to reach for her, as it is usually Colleen who reaches out. Arva waits. When she tires of waiting, she takes Colleen's wrist.

"I just don't like it." An undrugged Colleen is crying.

"What?"

"Forget it."

"I can't forget it. Just tell me."

Colleen lights Arva's candle. "That woman. That person who calls you here, who calls you at the bookstore. She must be your lover. You never mention her. It just makes me feel funny. I feel like I'm part of some triangle or something."

Arva looks at Colleen's unswollen face flickering while she tries to formulate an answer. Arva does not want to say, "That woman is two women." Arva does not want to mention Goldie. Arva does not want to remind either Colleen or herself that although they sleep together they are not lovers. So, Arva cups Colleen's chin in her hand and says, "You are not part of some triangle or something."

The two women laugh, and one of them blows out the candle.

Their pattern is broken by the passage of time and the appearance on the kitchen table of a passport issued to Colleen Harriston. Colleen has called a cab to take her to the airport, though Arva offered to drive. Arva waits with Colleen at the doorway down to Mother Right Bookstore.

Colleen hands the passport to Arva. "What a crappy picture. Take a look."

"Those pictures are always crappy."

Arva waits for Colleen to ask her about her own passport. Arva has a story about three different passports, all glued with her picture. Three different names issued by three different countries. These were among the things she found in her mother's locked drawer after her mother's death. When Arva found them, all she could say was, "Expecting another Holocaust, Mom?"

What she would not tell anyone, not even Colleen, not even if she asked, is that she tried to renew all three passports.

But Colleen does not ask Arva anything. Colleen thanks Arva "for everything." Colleen says she has learned a lot from Arva. Colleen says she will write. When Colleen sees the cab, she kisses Arva on the cheek and pulls her suitcase through the door.

That summer, Arva will receive a single postcard from Colleen. It will have a scene from Munich on the front and three lines of smeared writing on the back. Arva will tack it to the Mother Right bulletin board, at the back of the store, near the Lesbian Literature shelf.

# INTER/VIEWS

*CL: Let me ask you a standard question: What has influenced your work?*

*A: Oh, lots of things. LSD. God. The Goddess. The Triple Goddess. The lost goddesses. Jack Kerouac and the Beat Generation. Bob Dylan and Bob Marley and Baba Ram Dass. The Spinners. Mary Daly.*

*CL: Are there any visual artists who have had an impact on your painting?*

*A: Well, first let me say that my art isn't confined to painting. It's more of a mixed-media event. But let me see, visual artists. I've made it my business to try and acquaint myself with the lives of many visual artists—women visual artists. I admire them, but my work is very different, although I think it participates in that tradition. But as far as influence, well, that's hard to say. I guess I find it difficult to identify with them. I mean, Cassatt had Degas, Kahlo had Rivera, O'Keeffe had that old photographer guy. I've never had that sort of mentor, although I suppose we've all had mentors of one sort or another.*

REWIND. STOP. FAST FORWARD. STOP.

Transcribing is difficult. With no secretary and no secretarial skills, the progress of Clover Leach is painfully slow. She is also slowed this morning by an aggravating inability to make even the smallest decisions. What type of paper should she use? Lined or unlined? Legal or letter size? Yellow, or white, or that shade of buff recently purchased on a whim? And should she edit as she listened or transcribe it all, even though it was obvious that she could not include talk about LSD or goddesses in the weekly *Mirror?* But wouldn't it be better to have it all written out for the article she hoped to do, perhaps for something slick, like *Art in America?* And what initials should she use for her interviewee, a woman named, of all things, Seaglass? Just an *S*, looking so solitary and slightly profane? Surely *SG* was wrong, for hadn't she been told that it was *Seaglass, one word?* Perhaps just *Q* and *A* would do, but could Clover really do without the reward of her own initials?

There are so many details to care about, details too small to bother a better person, Clover thinks. The tiniest problems bloat until their solutions absorb the morning Clover tries to steal from a life which seems comprised solely of endless details. At noon, her sister-in-law would be bringing back Joshua. Clover had begged and bartered to have a morning free from her twenty-month-old son. It wasn't enough to have an interview due for the local paper, an interview that would pay her fifty dollars (less than her husband David could make in a fifteen-minute phone conversation, as he had told her—twice), an interview assigned to a relatively inexperienced free-lancer because none of the staff writers found it remotely desirable (and she was a free-lancer solely by the grace of David's connection with the publisher, as he didn't need to tell her, even once). No, this interview was not excuse enough to hire someone to watch Joshua, a practice acceptable if she accompanied David to a dinner or a party or even to a movie. So she concocted an illness, the flu or a possible case of food poisoning, something with lots of dizziness and vomiting, and prevailed on her husband's sister Gloria to take care of the difficult Joshua for a morning.

When Clover is away from Joshua, she does not think of him. She does not worry abut him or wonder what he is doing at that precise moment or hope that he is being good. Instead, she becomes preoccupied with her baby's father, her husband, David W. Leach.

David is like something beige and spongy in her mind, an ominous detail which never fails to expand to fill all the available space. Even as she tries to push thoughts of him away, to concentrate on Seaglass and the interview and the deadline, all thinking dissolves into questions about him.

Why had he, for example, gotten her this assignment, and then acted as if it were both a burden and a piece of pure fluff? Why had he volunteered a week before to watch Joshua the Saturday morning she had arranged to do the interview, only to get surly when she reminded him of his promise and begrudgingly agree to "babysit" his own son? Why did he smirk the few times she had mentioned the interview, imply that her "jaunt" had been tantamount to neglect of their son, taunt her about her "visit to that dyke"—acting as if this assignment was some evidence of lack of character on her part rather than an event arranged at his instigation? Why did he fear that she would be attracted to Seaglass, that she would fall into bed with her while the recorder whirred?

Alone on the bed she and David shared, where Joshua was conceived; alone, gloriously alone in her nightgown without the threat of its silly material being slid over her thigh, Clover pushes the buttons of the cassette recorder. She writes down every word with a fine-line black marker on a yellow legal pad, deciding not to confront more details than absolutely necessary.

*CL: Were you surprised when you were awarded a state grant in visual art?*
*A: A little, yes. It's the second time I'd applied, but I was encouraged to do it again by one of the previous committee members. My work is a little outside the expected unconventionality allowed to artists. It doesn't always photograph well because it's three-dimensional, so it's always risky sending representations of my work. And then there is the political content. It's usually quite feminist and, I like to think, quite anarchist as well. Things not exactly popular with state governments.*
PAUSE.

Seaglass is sitting on the beach, sitting on the sand without a blanket or towel, sitting watching the sun flare behind clouds in the east sky. Behind her, half-shrouded by low dunes, palmettos, pines, and buttonwood, sits her house. It is a house flanked to the north by a luxury resort and to the south by the public beach. It would be flattery to describe the house as excessively modest. It is virtually a shack, but it is a large shack haphazardly connected to the small shack she uses as a workroom. Seaglass has worked not only at her art, but to bring these structures into the protected ambit of compliance with the county building codes.

Every morning Seaglass slides out from the surf and every morning seems a miracle to Seaglass: the sunrise, the swim, the sitting. It seems no less than a miracle that she lives here, that she owns acres of land bordering on the Atlantic, that she has the freedom to practice her art. A miracle, she thinks, but an honest miracle. She has convinced herself of the integrity of her fortune because any contrivance would signal instability, something she can no longer bear. Not every morning, but more mornings than not, and this morning in particular, she reviews the highlights of the chain of events which brought her to her present state, as if she is checking for a weak link that she might need to repair.

Running away from home was precipitated, if not caused by, an episode in which she hid behind an olive-green armchair from her father and his widest belt. She was sixteen, and he was screaming *harlot*, that old-fashioned word which still presents itself to her as an image of a white-faced harlequin painted with black tears rather than as the more conventionally painted lady to which her father referred.

A year and seventeen hundred miles later, she met White in an emergency room of a local hospital. She'd cut her foot pretty badly, but not bad enough to warrant any immediate attention from the emergency room staff. They had their hands full, and had even called a cop to deal with a crazy old man attempting to sign himself out of the hospital. Then some hospital administrator came and declared that the old man would have to go into a nursing home unless someone could sign as being responsible for him. Suddenly she was saying she was his granddaughter, lying about being eighteen. The hospital administrator was unbelieving, yet relieved to be rid of the troublesome old man.

She drove White home to his place on the beach, bought when

he was pensioned from the railroad before World War II. He invited her to stay a while in case the cop came out to check up on things, and because he was a bit grateful, a bit curious, and had been a runaway himself. She was handy, a decent cook, responsible, and a good driver. She drove White to the post office, to the bank to deposit his federal checks, to the store to buy cases of Coca-Cola. She fixed up the shack until it became a house. She used the small hut to take up painting again, beginning to paint on pieces of wood or on the doors of junked cars. When the roof of the house needed a repair beyond the means of White's monthly checks, she got a job waitressing at a resort, ignorant of White's bank accounts.

He never asked her for her name, but began to call her Seaglass, because "the ocean smooths dangerous edges." Then he asked her to marry him. It was a deal, he said. She had to agree that he'd never go into a nursing home, that she'd kill him first. In return, she'd get the property when he died. He told her he had it all arranged with his lawyer. After the blood tests, she drove them to the attorney's office. She expected pages of contracts with clauses and exigencies and paragraphs she could not understand. Instead, the lawyer performed an abbreviated ceremony, had White sign a new deed which included her as his wife and equal owner, and had White execute a simple will. After it was over, the lawyer asked to speak with her a moment. She was not shocked by his words, for she knew how things appeared. "I hope you know how much he trusts you, and how much I hope that trust is not misplaced," was what the lawyer said.

Seaglass didn't wait for White to die. He never hindered her freedom, for she had no desire to go far. She'd been places enough. The library, the post office, the grocery store, the lumberyard, and once in a while the woman's bar were her destinations. He did not comment on any of the women who would occasionally spend the night with her out in what she now called her studio. He watched wrestling, drank too many Cokes while mourning that they sure weren't what they used to be, and pretended to eat more than he did of the soup or the chicken or the fish that she made him. When he died, sixteen years later at the age of ninety-one, she grieved. She had him cremated and threw his ashes into the sea. She likes to think she swims with him every morning, although she had never known him to put as much as a toe into the ocean.

*CL: Did you come from an artistic family or background?*
*A: No, not at all. Actually, it's exactly the opposite. Visual art was my way of rebelling, I guess. Both my parents are blind, you see, so I was never encouraged in that direction or exposed to any visual art. But I was also very free. I mean, I drew lots when I was a kid and no one was there to tell me that the sun wasn't blue or that the ocean wasn't pink. My brothers and sisters are all younger. So, by the time I got to school, I was what they called incorrigible. I flunked Art twice, for refusing to follow instructions. Then they called in the school psychologist, who thought my fascination with art—I was drawing all the time by then—was odd, and that the pictures I was producing were marks of a disturbed kid. So they scheduled a conference with my parents, and when they realized they were blind, well, that seemed to explain everything to them. They left me alone after that. Then my father became president of the Federation of the Blind and we moved to the state capital. When I went to high school there, I was considered talented. Then I ran away.*
STOP. FAST FORWARD. REWIND. STOP.

Clover always tries to do twenty things at once. It is more than a habit, such as oiling one's legs every night or picking one's lip. It is more a survival mechanism, a protective coloring. It's as if she believes that by doing enough things at the same time, no one will notice if she sneaks one or two she does solely for herself into the overgrown environment of the things she does for other people.

Never mind that the only person there to notice anything this morning is Joshua. He rolls a ball back and forth on the tropical tan couch while Clover fidgets with the recorder, rereads her notes, does the laundry, makes a grocery list, tries not to burn butterscotch pudding in a double boiler, listens for the phone to ring, and fixes the kitchen clock. As soon as Clover gathers her concentration on the interview, Joshua shrieks and makes a demand.

Clover would be happy to satisfy each and every one of Joshua's demands, all the parental advice books be damned, if only she could understand what her son wanted. She thinks he should be talking by now. She thinks that every mother should understand her child, that there should be at least some sort of crude communication system between them, even if it is unintelligible to all others. Clover thinks that when a child says *bak*, a mother knows that this means *chocolate milk* or *take a walk* and not *banana*, or *rum cake*, or *go to hell*. She thinks every other mother in the world possesses this magic, every mother except her.

It does occur to her that this might be just another fragment in that oversized myth of maternal instinct. It is difficult for her to credit an instinct of which she has never been personally afforded even the tiniest sign. All through her pregnancy she was convinced she carried a daughter. Her conviction allowed her to endure David, and David's sister, and David's mother and father, and David's golf buddies and business partners, and every other person who expressed the belief that David's first child would be a boy, as if another gender were not merely unthinkable but impossible.

Equally impossible is any notion that the child might be less than perfect. Labor had been induced, painful, and fruitless, finally ending in a caesarean. The doctor's discussion concentrated on her choice of swimming attire, her "bikini cut," more than anything remotely medical. Her failure to birth the child—and it seemed to be looked upon as *her* failure—was the justification of both the family and the family physicians for Clover's preoccupation with some defect in the child. Clover thinks a mother should know, but also knows that her misgivings have no weight, especially when balanced against the pronouncements of David's family and their doctors.

"Perfectly normal, strong, and healthy," the members of David's family say, as if in a chorus. Though it seems to Clover that the time each of them spends with Joshua is as short as the rotating doctors' perfunctory checkup every third time Joshua gets his scheduled inoculations from a nurse. It also seems to Clover that David's family devotes all of their sparse moments with the child to an inspection and ensuing discussion of whether he looks like a Leach.

It is during such times that Clover misses her mother the most, not only because her mother would stand as living proof of an entirely different bloodline, but also because her mother would sneak her a smile at the name Leach. And though she never would, Clover can imagine confiding to her mother the appropriateness of Joshua's last name: for he is pale and sluggish and siphons blood from her like an outdated panacea.

She likes to imagine that she could slough off her guilt by talking with her mother; guilt not from the birth event, but from her failure to love Joshua enough. Her guilt is compounded by her conviction that the child knows everything, including her resentment of the way he connects her to the bloodsuckers of David's family. Since this is her fantasy, her fantasy mother does not remind her of inconvenient facts, as her real mother most certainly would. Clover had chosen to marry David, to take his name, to stay in this small coastal town where his family grows like vines from their founding-father ancestor—and she had done all these things long enough to know better before submitting to the expectation that she become pregnant, as if motherhood could bestow upon her the status, the freedom, that she had onced hoped marriage would.

*CL: What are you working on now?*
*A: Several things. I'm thinking of doing a series on women and religion. Now, there's something where my family background definitely comes into play. I used to escort my mother to three different churches every Sunday morning, and she'd cry through the services, except for the sermon. All that has got to affect a child. I did love the music, the stained-glass windows, the decoration of the pulpit for different seasons, and the smell of the wood. But anyway, at the moment I'm finishing a sort of free-standing collage entitled,* Our Lady of Florida Casts Down Her Eyes to Bless Her Fruits, Her Daughters, and Her Children. *A long title, I know, but I'm paying more attention to titles these days. There really is an Our Lady of Florida, you know. It's a monastery, I think. Anyway, there's a statue down on U.S. 1. I think stuff like that is almost unbelievable. Of course, my piece is quite a bit different from that traditional religious icon, though my piece is religious, too, but it has some other sources. The downcast eyes— have you ever seen one of those huge statues of Buddha? You think the eyes are half-closed until you stand beneath them and see them almost glowing right at you. It's real mystical. I fell in love with Buddha when I was kid on a field trip to a museum in New York. I want to make my* Lady of Florida *that way: beneath her eyes is every question and every answer. And the fruit—fruit is very religious as well. And of course daughters and children. I love children. I love fruit.*

*I live on fruit.*
PAUSE.

There's a storm at sea. The sun is climbing over whitecaps which stretch to the horizon, as if pieces of low-flung clouds are being licked by the rolling tongues of the ocean. Seaglass wanders along the shore, looking for molted feathers. She washes each feather in the surf while trying to determine the bird of its origin, then smooths all the barbs until the vane is velvety. She examines the shaft and quill for sturdiness. If the feather is less than perfect, she does not discard it, but simply notes the defect. Feathers are not rare on this beach still thickly populated with royal terns and brown pelicans and dotted with egrets and herons. Yet the search for a flawless feather would be futile. Besides, Seaglass concludes, the hair of *Our Lady of Florida* should not be made of faultless feathers, but of ones that had flown.

Once she had wanted, more than anything, to be able to fly: to fly away from her parents' narrow house where the radio in each room trumpeted a religious program, or a baseball game, or music so outdated Seaglass refused to acknowledge that she recognized it. Now her desires are more pedestrian. She wants to be able to walk on the sand leaving the shallowest footprints humanly possible, to complete *Our Lady of Florida* in time for the show of the five grant winners in Tallahassee, to have a one-woman show somewhere, and to call Clover.

The desire to talk with Clover again surprises her. She turns it over and over in her mouth, expecting it to taste like grass, to feel soft as a hill where foals test their strength, but it is harder and sharper, like metal, like silver. The anticipation of the interview had been unpleasant, but she'd been disarmed by Clover's interest and had spoken more to her than to anyone she could ever remember, saying things she had never before verbalized. She sat in the Holiday Inn restaurant on a Saturday morning, saying whatever entered her head. She wants to talk to her again, but she also wants a chance to be able to ask Clover a few questions, to have her to reveal herself and her ideas.

Seaglass knows a more impulsive woman would get to a phone and call, saying something like, "Well, it just occurred to me you can't very well write an introduction to the interview without seeing my studio"; or, "There are some things I've forgotten to tell you, would you care to come over and walk on the beach?"; or, "I'm almost finished with that new piece I told you about. Why don't you come see it?" But Seaglass has never been impulsive. Even her running away from home or marrying a man almost sixty years older than herself had not been impulsive acts. Before she acts she needs to be clear about her motives, which at the moment seem to her as sandy as the small tidal pool from which she picks a slate tail feather.

It isn't sex, she thinks, or it isn't just sex. Just sex is her adolescent boyfriend biting at her neck, her clavicle, her breasts. Just sex is picking up a woman, having a great time, but never suggesting another encounter. Just sex is giving an elderly man a blow job, when both parties are wise enough not to take such things seriously. No, she thinks, this is more than attraction or convenience or boredom. This is serious. She washes another feather in the salt water.

*CL: What are your plans for the future? Do you have any particular goals?*
*A: Plans for the future? I don't really know. I mean, I want to keep working, to finish* Our Lady of Florida, *to complete the terms of the state arts grant, and just to do more work. Like I told you, I'm conceptualizing a series on women in religion, so I've got a few more ideas for that—things I really can't talk about yet. As far as goals, well, I guess my ultimate goal would be to expand visual art beyond the visual, if that makes any sense. When you asked me about influences before, I think that's what I was trying to get at: music, literature, breaking down how we've compartmentalized the five senses, and of course, adding that sixth sense. But I've got no real concrete plans to go anywhere or anything like that. I'm not that kind of person.* STOP.

It is one of those thoughts that creeps from the sleeping mind into the morning, not really a dream, not even a vision, but a statement. It is an intuition in the form of a statement, a self-realization which harbors no judgment. For Clover, it comes as she untangles Joshua's high-pitched screech from the cry of a laughing gull. For Clover, it comes as a simple sentence she repeats out loud, oblivious of the soundly sleeping man spread across three-fourths of the bed.

"I wish there were something wrong with him."

She means her baby, Joshua. She pulls her words after her like a shredding kite not constructed for the low swift winds that make the moon seem to cling high in the morning sky. Comforting her child, she reels in her battered emotions, unwinding them again only after Joshua is fed, David is gone, and she is looking for the Seaglass transcript. Like an eleven-year-old alone in her parents' house for almost the first time, she talks out loud, honestly and to herself, of things she cannot quite admit.

"I wonder where that damn transcript got to. It isn't that I want anything to be *wrong* with Josh, I just want some explanation. He's an odd kid. No one else notices, but he's strange. There must be some reason. A reason would show David and the rest of that pompous family that they aren't always right, that they aren't perfect. And if there were a reason, then I would know Josh really doesn't hate me. It would be easier to love him."

Doesn't she love him now? she demands of herself, but she lets herself off the hook of her question to continue her quest for the missing transcript. She doesn't know now that the transcript is useless, that she will edit it and submit it only to have it returned by the editor saying he wanted a profile, like the one on that local kid who placed third in the State Science Fair by building an echo chamber. Clover doesn't yet know that the interview will never be published, so she searches for her sloppily written pages from a yellow legal pad. She entertains a vague notion that she is on a treasure hunt. The old chest will not contain gold doubloons, but accomplishment, independence, and an elusive state she embodies with a sun-splattered image of Seaglass.

She continues to marvel at what she sees as the artist's guiltless freedom and the fact that her parents were blind. These two issues seem to Clover to be inextricably bound, knotted into a secret which could explode a small universe. It is this knot which Clover wants to weigh in her hands, not to untie it, but merely to examine it with her fingertips as one would casually rub the kitchen countertops in a new house. Yes, she thinks, I would like to live in the hub of that knot, to take Joshua there and let him grow bounded only by that loose perfection.

Joshua, unaware of his mother's mystical plans, is playing with a box of 108 crayons. He is not coloring, but arranging the crayons: separating the oranges from the reds from the yellows. Clover stops her ferreting to play with Joshua. She is impressed with his visual acuity, but wonders whether it is unusual enough in a child his age to warrant her reaction. Perhaps Seaglass would know something like that, she thinks, either ignoring or ignorant of the fact that the life of Seaglass does not include children. Yet because Clover always errs on the side of the ordinary, even while she lusts for the exceptional, she is not satisfied with Joshua's accomplishment. She holds up a crayon and reads the name from the label, inviting Joshua to repeat. "Salmon," she says. Then, "magenta." Supposing these are too difficult, she finds blue and then green and then black. The child is silent, until he squeals wildly as if she is stealing his crayons, disturbing his patterns, corrupting his art. Well, he certainly isn't blind, she thinks, putting the crayons back into his rows.

The worst way to find something missing is to look for it. Her mother taught her this. It will turn up. She will remember where she put the transcript, and if she doesn't, she can always make another one. The latter alternative will mean a lot of work wasted, but it will also provide an excuse for her to listen to the vibrant voice of Seaglass again. She resolves to devote the remainder of the morning to Joshua. Perhaps she can show him how to color. But the child isn't in the living room with his crayons, which are now scattered across the carpet. Maybe he's found the transcript, she thinks with a smile, until she sees him in her bedroom, the drawer of the nightstand open. Joshua is standing almost three-feet tall with yards and yards of cassette tape unraveled around him on the floor. His index finger fits perfectly in one of the two holes in the cassette tape, and he is turning, turning.

The phone is ringing, but Clover cannot hear it because she is screaming. She is screaming at Joshua from the bottom of her lungs. She is screaming as if, suddenly, her life depended on being heard. The phone is ringing, but Joshua cannot hear it. Not because his mother is screaming so loud that it would be impossible to hear even his own heart beating, but because he is deaf.

# ARTICHOKE HEARTS

## RAPIDLY BOILING WATER

Steam coats the windows and condenses into perfectly romantic droplets of water.

It is the type of transformation for which my soul longs.

It is the type of transformation which my intellect avoids.

I melt butter in someone else's kitchen, in the company of three other white women, two of whom I engage with in more than occasional, always secret, sexual liaisons. I try to remember that my relationships are *discrete* rather than *secret*, but a change of phrase doesn't prevent me from being curious about whether I've betrayed only one, or more likely two, or possibly all three of the women in the room.

As I watch the droplets dramatically descend to the sill over the kitchen sink, I conclude I've betrayed everyone—including myself.

The water rapidly boils around artichokes green as frogs. If the artichokes were frogs, they would have jumped out when dropped in the steaming water. However, live frogs will stay in once-cool water if the temperature is raised gradually enough, until the frogs boil to death. I think this experiment is a great moral lesson, but when I try to apply it to my own life, my only conclusion is to jump.

The artichokes remain in the pot until they soften.

The women sit on slatted chairs around the dining room table. It is round, made of laminated wood, and smells of Murphy (*pure vegetable*) Oil Soap—the cleaner I had recommended and with which I had routinely cleaned this table myself. I've routinely cleaned many tables, but this table had once been mine. When a married woman whose house I clean (and whose bed I've shared on a few sunny afternoons) gave me a birch dining set, I gave this table to my friend: a friend I either sleep with or betray, or both.

There is meatless lasagna (at least two other women are vegetarians).

There is bread brought from the local food co-op where I used to work, before I started my free-lance house cleaning business.

There are wildflowers of deep lavender I picked on my way here, on my way from spending the night out past the land co-op.

There are artichokes, huge and sharp, on each plate. Each woman plucks at her leaves. We dip each leaf into the proud centerpiece of a bowl of melted butter. We slide each leaf through our teeth, stealing glances at each other.

I want conversation to mitigate all those glances. So I wonder aloud about the first person to eat an artichoke. "They seem so threatening," I say.

This is a favorite theme of mine: threatening fruits and vegetables. My favorite example in this favorite theme is pineapple. Imagine the first person to eat a pineapple.

"Oh, Shelia, the first person to eat an artichoke was probably an herbalist," she says, in her best butch voice, "but imagine the first person to drink cow's milk."

She is as queer and as gay as the rest of us, but the only one old enough to remember the days of difference between those two terms. I try to remember the last time, if there was one, that I slept with her.

"I don't think cow's milk is strange at all." A drop of butter settles on my breast. I try to decide whether I should stick my fingers in my water glass and rub my shirt before it stains. I decide against bringing up pineapples, hoping to change the subject back to silence.

Then someone winks at me.

Then someone else.

"Do you want your heart?"

"No, I like only the leaves."

"Yes, the leaves are the real delicacy."

I promise myself to stay out of conversations so susceptible to subterranean meanings, but someone leans at me, saying, "Well, Sheila, I guess that means we get to devour their hearts."

Another wink from another eye.

I practice not being paranoid. It can't be true that all my secrets, I mean discretions—I guess I mean indiscretions—are exposed by this candle flame rapidly drowning in wax.

"Which part is the choke?" I do not voice this question and I do not respond to it.

Someone glances at someone else.

The silence squeaks like damp glass.

"More wine, bread, lasagna...," I finally answer, asking.

# THE WORLD'S LARGEST PIZZA

"Sheila," she says "you're the only person I can tell this to. You're such a sexual pluralist."

I am wary when anyone starts a sentence with my name. Equally wary when I'm the only one in the world who deserves to hear something. Even more wary when someone categorizes my sexuality. But wary or not, I love gossip, especially if it doesn't involve me.

It is Saturday. I've been cleaning my own apartment, for a change. It smells better than it looks.

She's been crying. "It's a man," she says.

She was one of the first dykes I met when I moved to this town three years ago, and she's still one of my favorites. I like her so much I've never slept with her. But as she tells me how it happened, tells me how she felt alone and needed something she calls "the solace of intimacy," tells me how there was no one she'd *really* been attracted to in weeks, maybe months, I want to retroactively volunteer my services. I want to ask her why she did not come to me with her loneliness and her milky freckled shoulders. I still think I can be all things to all women. I suppress a feeling of rejection that rises in my throat.

"I'm hungry. Have you eaten?"

"I can't eat," she says.

"You've got to eat. Let's go for pizza at Anthony's or Antonio's or Angelo's. Whatever that place is that puts the artichokes on the special vegetarian. You know, the restaurant that did the world's largest pizza and put pepperoni all over it."

Once in the restaurant booth, under a photograph of a man standing next to eleven thousand pounds of flour, she is silent. I am waiting.

"That isn't the worst of it," she says.

We order the vegetarian special, with double artichokes, double mushrooms, and ricotta cheese.

"He's married," she says.

"To a woman?" I ask.

"Yes. I guess I'll have a hard time maintaining my sisterhood quotient."

I am impressed with the seriousness of her plight. I've been involved with one or two men, and more than a few married women, although I've sworn off both. But I've never become even momentarily entangled with a married man: I'm not *that* pluralistic. It seems positively clichéd. It seems too outrageous for even the most outrageous lesbian.

"That isn't the worst of it," she says, again.

The pizza arrives. Ricotta like curdled cow's milk perches on leaves of heavily processed artichokes, which will be displeasingly smooth to the tongue.

"I know his wife. We've had dinner together."

"Recently?"

"As recently as last night. I left her, went home, and then he came over."

"What's she like?" I ask, not knowing what else to say.

"Sort of mousy. Very, very straight. She sort of clings to him. She told me she thinks she might be pregnant. I mean, really." She sounds very indignant. "She treats me like I'm her friend. I guess I do feel sorry for her. Ursa is just not the kind of woman I could be friends with."

"Ursa? She doesn't work at the food co-op, does she?"

"Yes, one of those women," she says, apparently forgetting that I once belonged in that category.

I stuff a triangle of pizza too far into my mouth, hoping to remain casual. But it's too much. I start coughing, virtually inhaling an artichoke leaf which sticks in my throat, on the inside of the spot where Ursa had kissed my neck for the last time when I told her I just had to swear off married women.

## THANKSGIVING

Being alone is my solution to a problem I can't define.

It isn't just that I can't decide who to be with, or that I really don't want to grace any discrete relationship with holiday status, or that I'm a vegetarian.

And it isn't that I fear rejection so much that I can't issue an invitation, or that I haven't gotten any invitations. In fact, I've got seven invitations for today, including one from a sexy single woman executive whose Tudor house I recently cleaned, and excluding the annual feast at the food co-op.

Raindrops collect on the outside of my apartment window. I feel singular and satisfied.

I want to enjoy my day.

I watch the parade on television while I sew a new zipper into my favorite black pants.

I take a shower until the hot water runs out.

I make a shopping list, knowing I can't fill it because the stores are closed.

The phone rings, and I don't answer it.

I examine my eyebrows, the healing of my recently sprained toe, a collection of mail I've been meaning to sort.

The phone rings again. I unplug it.

At about four, the sky still dark with rain, I realize I've been hungry for hours. I go to the cabinet, stocked with my usual groceries: a diversity of pasta products; jars of marinara sauce, mushrooms, and applesauce; cans of corn, artichokes, and pineapples.

I don't feel like boiling water for pasta, so I content myself with a bottle of B & B (*broiled in butter*) mushrooms and a can of Progresso (*product of Spain*) artichoke hearts. I pour them in a shallow bowl together. Reading the labels as I eat, always on the lookout for words like *beef fat*, I note that although the mushroom label does not approximate the number of mushrooms, the artichoke can promises *8-10*.

I count only six, knowing I've eaten only one. I imagine the scene

at the grocery store (not the food co-op, which sells only fresh artichokes). I've been swindled! I would cry. The missing artichoke heart
ruined my Thanksgiving dinner.

I like to imagine things I would never do: I do not make scenes.

There's a knock at the door. I feel a bit embarrassed by my jar
and can at the table, but there isn't time for camouflage.

It's Doreen. She's holding three camellias. They are too white
and do not smell.

"For you," she says, with a flourish.

We have been lovers. I remember this. Perhaps as briefly as one
night, but I remember. She is a woman who seduces me with the
raw edge of her need. She never acts tough, which unnerves me.

I follow her into the kitchen, offer her a glass of water, a mushroom, an artichoke.

But she wants to talk about us, about me. How we should be
together on holidays. How I shouldn't be alone.

I ask her what she did, trying to forestall the inevitable.

"I went to Ursa's. Some other women were there. There was a
turkey and stuffing. Some woman with freckles brought frog legs."

"Oh, I thought Ursa would be at the co-op."

"The food co-op is closing."

I pick up the empty can and start reading. I don't mean to be
rude, but my eye catches the phrase *first drain and halve artichoke
hearts*. I have done neither. I have failed to follow instructions yet again.

Doreen stand up, looking at me as if I'm very, very far away.

"You know," she says, knowing I don't, "we discussed you today
at dinner. Someone said you were a sexual pluralist. Someone else
said you were just a bitch. And do you know what I said?"

It would be impolite and untrue to say I didn't care. I love gossip,
even when it's about me. I nod in what I hope is a noncommittal way.

"I said you had a heart like—"

"Oh no," I say, "I can't bear the predictable."

"Glass," she continues.

And I can't help laughing as she sits back down, piercing a
processed choke with my fork.

When I finish reading the label, I will kiss her throat.

# PATERNITY

Her mind had a place it kept its secrets. The place was like a pocket in the tightest pair of jeans. The jeans were like those she had pulled on when she heard her father's key in the door on Saturday mornings. The pocket was like the one into which she'd carefully slip the bill her father would give her from his gambling winnings. Sometimes it was only a dollar bill. Usually it was a five or a ten, and rarely it was a twenty. It all depended on how her father's luck had run the night before, or so he said. He always gave her mother several bills. Once she saw him give her mother a hundred-dollar bill.

No matter how much money there was to hand out, her father always brought home fresh custard doughnuts and bloodshot eyes. She would break open a warm doughnut and watch her father's weary face transform as he told of the night's exploits. It wasn't just bragging, she knew, for her father was what they called a card-counter, and a good one. He was not a compulsive gambler, but a man blessed with a mathematical mind and cursed with the absence of opportunities that might provide other outlets for this talent. His only problem with gambling was finding people to bet against a white man who always seemed to win, a man who earned distrust because he did not drink or smoke.

She'd eat too many doughnuts, and her jeans would get tighter and tighter. She'd make her father a second and then a third cup of coffee. As she got older, she'd look at the man on the other side of the table and wonder if people were right when they said she was the spitting image of her father. It was hard for her to tell. He was such a *man*, with his blond crewcut, his angular six-foot-six frame, his large hands scarred by machines, and his hard blue eyes that bulged like frogs' eyes when he was angry. She couldn't imagine that she'd look like him when she grew up. After all, though her father was fairly handsome, he'd look pretty ugly as a woman in a culture which admired delicate women.

The intensity of her speculations would dissolve during the remainder of Saturday's routine. Her father would go to bed, reading the newspaper until he fell asleep. Her mother would leave for a half-day of overtime at the shirt factory. Kyla would be left alone with her list of chores.

Washing clothes was what she hated most. There was always a crowd in the basement laundry of the apartment building. No matter how thoroughly she thought she'd checked the pockets, it seemed that a stray piece of paper or tissue would predictably make its appearance known in the wash. She tried to clean out the washing machine as casually as possible, hoping that none of the fretting women in the small, hot room would notice. But even if they did not see the inside of the machine, it would be hard to ignore the paper shredded all over the wet clothes.

Kyla's children are waking her up by putting their fingers in her nose, in her mouth, in her ears. She usually enjoys sleep like a good cleaning, but today she wakes up feeling tired and dirty. Pieces of dreams still cling to her like shreds of soggy tissue. Her secrets often tumble out of their pocket in the watery world of sleep.

"You kids," she says, trying to be stern. Yet she is already smiling, already putting the names and faces of the night behind her. She finds it difficult to resist admiring her children, as Rachel, Donovan, and Marina giggle and exchange the conspiratorially innocent looks of creatures still seeking workable vocabulary. She kisses and cuddles each of them in turn, but in no particular order, and then all of them together. They tumble around, laughing and shrieking, Kyla thankful that she invested in the queen-size bed that often supports four sleeping bodies for at least part of the night.

Breakfast is luxurious, and Kyla is thankful again, although she thinks the world is unfair for defining the simple pleasures of life as luxuries. There are fresh strawberries and lush pieces of whole-wheat toast with homemade apple butter and the chatter of children with food on their faces. There are curtainless kitchen windows, open to admit the tropical February breeze and the glimpses of red and pink hibiscus waving to the sun. There is the humming of her own washing machine in the garage and a selection of New Age music on the public radio station. Kyla wants to know why everyone can't live like this—and she isn't interested in hearing economic theories. The music seeping from the stereo's one working speaker is enough theory to digest this morning.

Then there is the colorful rush of getting four human beings outfitted for one day: matching socks, a pair of striped cotton overalls to iron, a purple barrette for the baby's hair, rainbow shoelaces tied in double knots, and the search for the missing red shirt. Scurries to the car, a short ride, kisses good-bye, and Kyla is pulling back into the alley with only the baby, Marina, in the carseat. The older two children have started their day, equipped with lunch boxes and new beeswax modeling clay, at the Free Hearts Alternative School.

Kyla and Marina do not enter their stucco house from the same door they exited. Instead, they walk from the wide gravel driveway around to the front of the house where they are greeted by a huge wood-burnished sign: KYLA DADE, C.P.A. The office is windowed, neither small nor large, neither neat or disheveled, with a few framed photographs of children scattered on the wall among the diplomas and political posters. The slightly rusted baby swing welcomes Marina, who watches as Kyla flicks on the computer and sifts through the account books and tax forms on a long wooden table. Kyla puts on her glasses and begins to work on the pitiful income statements of Spectrum, a cooperative art gallery whose members are contemplating Kyla's suggestion to apply for nonprofit status.

The brass bells tied to the door serve their purpose at about half-past two, while Kyla is breastfeeding Marina and eating a slice of date bread piled with cream cheese. It is Rose, of Rose's Paper Works, a small shop near the ocean selling handmade paper, novelty notecards, and postcards by local artists. Rose is one of Kyla's few clients whose business shows a substantial profit. Kyla considers it one of the limitations of her present life that Rose is also one of her best friends.

"What's up? I just thought I'd stop in on my way to the shop from Nita's. Nita and I were just talking about you and the children. What a wonderful mother you are. How brave you are to do what you're doing all by yourself. And," Rose pauses to smooth the backs of her hands under her shoulder-length hair and flip it in the humid air, "how your children look so much alike."

Kyla attempts the time-tested diversionary tactic of offering libations, in this case, a cup of tea, with a litany of choices including Rose's favorite, orange blossom. No matter how often it happens, Kyla is startled when Rose chooses to divulge gossip to its subject. Kyla knows that people talk about her. After all, she and the children inhabit a close community in a tourist trap on the southern tip of Florida. Kyla also knows that although she is respected for the fees she keeps reasonable with her unerring efficiency, and the services she performs with her unremitting reliability, she is considered slightly inferior because she is not an artist. Her art of accounting is disparaged, as if it is merely a technical skill. There is no one in this town who shares Kyla's conviction about the magical nature of numbers, no one here who understands the mystery of Kyla's favorite numbers—three and seven. The numbers that have guided her course in life. The numbers that were always the solution to her father's, "I'm thinking of a number from one to ten." It was just a matter of choosing which one of the two, and her father usually allowed her guess to be correct.

"Of course, you know that everyone in town wonders. I mean it's only natural." Rose sips her steeping tea. "And I wonder what will happen when this man finally appears to claim the fruits of his seed."

"Life is not like a soap opera."

"Oh, I don't know about that. I had a friend in New York who used to write for one of those things. All she did was read the newspaper and remember her childhood. Have you ever watched any? Some of those daytime dramas are very realistic."

"You mean the scenes where the darling little boy—who has aged five years in two weeks while no one else has gotten any older—has survived a terrible car crash and needs several gallons of a rare type of blood and the hospital loudspeaker blares for the *real* father of little Jeffrey Robinson to report immediately to the operating room and all the doctors and nurses raise their left eyebrows at each other?"

Rose laughs but is undaunted. "I guess you're right. Men just don't care about kids." Kyla doesn't remember saying that, but she lets Rose continue. "I mean, I never knew my father. He left my mother when we were kids. I hated him. I saw him once when I was twenty and I couldn't even look at the bastard."

Kyla has heard this story before, from Rose and from a hundred other adults whose voices receded into childhood tones when they talked about the desertion of their fathers. Then there were those who talked about the emotional distance of their fathers, as if they were men with hollow bodies. It all made Kyla vaguely defensive, as if she should rush to protect the institution of fatherhood.

"That must have been difficult," Kyla tries to sound sympathetic.

"Oh, I survived. What was your father like?"

"My father is a nice guy, regular salt of the earth. He was always good to me, still is. Nothing traumatic in our relationship. Kind of boring, actually."

"Well, I always suspected as much. But while we're trading secrets," Rose persists, despite the downward turn of Kyla's full lips, "why don't you just tell me the truth. Your children all have the same father, don't they?" Rose sits back, as pleased as if she thought her bland invocation would be sufficient to convince a pathological liar to make an exception, a guiltless sinner to confess.

"What makes you think that?"

"They all look so much alike."

They look like me." Kyla is exactly right. The four people share the same pale coloring, the same honey-streaked curling hair, the same eyes round as blue moons and protruding from the oval angularity of their faces. Their lips are uniformly even and full, their noses aquiline, their fingers long, and their hands disproportionately large.

"That's true," Rose admits, only slightly hiding her disappointment, "though they must have inherited something from their father— or fathers."

"Not if they don't have any." Kyla rocks Marina, pressing their faces close together like a nineteenth-century painting of mother and child.

The day rapidly collapses around Kyla as if Rose had started a landslide. When Kyla loses interest in her clients' fiscal tax years, she tries to edit her computer program on nonprofit corporations. Marina's whining distracts her, and she overwrites the program, losing three-days work. Free Heart School telephones to announce that Donovan has had another "accident." Can she please bring a change of clothes, and is she really sure that he is toilet trained sufficiently to be in the preschool? Kyla dutifully bustles Marina into the compact blue station wagon to deliver a shirt and pair of overalls for her son, but then decides to take both Donovan and Rachel back home, in the hopes of an early and quiet evening.

The children have a different agenda. They bicker and demand Kyla's absolute attention. Marina cries. Rachel pours the dog's bowl of water over Donovan's head. Marina spits up. Donovan pulls the training pants from his dresser drawer and puts them in the toilet. Marina screams. All three children want only to cling to Kyla.

A sweet supper does not console them. Attempted treats of bowls of ice cream, favorite books, Lego blocks, forbidden pastel chalks, blowing bubbles, and coloring books are useless against their ill tempers. The usually enjoyed communal bath only results in six round blue eyes which bulge and stare at Kyla as if she is a traitor to some cause to which she does not know she should belong. It feels a hundred hours past midnight when she outlasts her children's burst of tyranny and the children are finally asleep in their own small beds, seeming to listen to each other's cranky breathing, waiting for the signal to renew the mutiny.

It is one of those nights Kyla cries from exhaustion. It is one of those nights when the joy of stretching diagonally across her queen-size bed is not enough. She wants someone to gently move her over as he comes to bed after checking the children. It is one of those nights Kyla doubts her choices and curses the career that gives her the freedom to implement her schemes. She wishes the phone would ring with a rescue message. The problem Kyla has tonight, like all such nights, is that she cannot decide who should be the bearer of the message. She knows that it would be a man, and that he would look enough like her to be her twin brother.

Only in her fitful sleep does Kyla allow specific men to be contenders for the role of rescuer. She has dreams about pulling a list of three names from her jeans, rejecting each one, then folding the list carefully and slipping it into her tight pocket as she reaches for another custard doughnut.

When the phone finally rings with a would-be rescue message rather than a client or a request for Kyla to volunteer at the battered women's shelter, it is weeks later and weeks too late. Things have been running extraordinarily smoothly. Donovan hasn't had an accident in all of March. Rachel has learned to love reading aloud to her brother and sister. Marina is sleeping through the night. Kyla's accounts are in order, and the income tax deadline is approaching gracefully. Kyla is spending less time with Rose and more time with Evelyn, a new and more considerate friend.

Besides, it is early spring and the weather is heavenly. It is the season which makes the populations of the northern sections of the country plunder their address books for acquaintances in the sub-tropics who wouldn't mind a visitor or two. All of Kyla's children were born in winter.

Douglas is on the other end of Kyla's long-distance line, and he wants to visit. He and Kyla have been friends for a long time. They met each other in college, years before Douglas went north to Mackinac Island at the strait between the icy lakes of Michigan and Huron, and Kyla came south to a narrow strip of land off the Gold Coast of Florida. Yet there are certain old lovers one should never trust: lovers who left living scabs rather than mending wounds. She is trying to remember her vow never to see Douglas again. And Kyla is suspicious because he is now married.

Douglas has a charm that penetrates while it implies that he needs to talk to Kyla about family problems only she will understand. The wary Kyla tosses her hair generously, and somewhat flirtatiously, and tells him she'll pick him up at the airport next Tuesday. She puts her better judgment to sleep like a naughty child.

That child gets restless once Douglas is actually in her presence. Her real children seem to overwhelm him at first with their busy corporeality, but by the time the troupe arrives at the stucco house facing west, Douglas is easy with the kids and they all seem to like him. He loves children and tells Kyla this fact over and over on the ride from the airport, as if it is not obvious, as if it contains some deeper message. Kyla is carefully registering her perceptions. She is open to a conclusion that he gives any one child extra attention.

Kyla shows Douglas the guest room, its demure twin beds outfitted with pink and sea green-striped sheets that look fresh as the first squeeze from a new tube of toothpaste. He laughs and strokes her head. Once she had called him *oenomel,* an ancient Greek beverage made of wine and honey, something that is both strong and sweet. She was studying the classics then, fascinated with the ancient Greeks and their myriad theories about the perfect number. He was studying French literature and used to read her Flaubert in his faltering rendition of the original. Now he sells hand-hammered silver to tourists on a summer resort island that allows no cars. He married a former Paris fashion model. Now she delves into columns of numbers, making sure each is accurate, if not perfect. She is an unwed mother three times. The small ironies of life are not wasted on either of them.

It takes him two days to tell her he is disturbed because his wife Lenore is sterile. He tells her this after her own three children are safely asleep and it is just two adults sitting on the back step listening for the distant sound of sloshing salt water. It seems Lenore knew she could not conceive, but did not tell Douglas because she thought he wouldn't marry her. Douglas is weeping. "Deception," he says, "always makes me this way."

"Kyla, I want to know. I need to know."

"Come on. We've got to get going. Your plane leaves near midnight."

"I can't leave until you tell me."

"Evelyn's already on her way over to stay with the kids."

"Kyla, don't be so cruel. I've got to know, is Donovan my child?"

"Ssh. The children are sleeping. And I told you, he's not. Now don't be ridiculous."

"It's not ridiculous. We were lovers the last time I came down. He looks enough like me to be mine, doesn't he?"

"Look, let me tell you in plain English. I got my period after we fucked the last time. You aren't Donovan's father. You aren't Rachel's or Marina's father either." Kyla notices that she has lapsed into the harsh tones of her childhood neighborhood, tones her father never used, tones which meant the speaker was either lying through her teeth or telling a horrible truth.

"This is serious. Very serious. Because if Donovan isn't my child, I'm going to have to divorce Lenore. I mean, I've always wanted children. I've always thought I'd have at least one child somewhere in the world. I don't want to hurt Lenore, but I've got no choice."

"I don't understand. If you suddenly found out you were a father by some woman other than Lenore, you'd stay with Lenore?" Kyla is stifling her soft laugh, reminded of soap operas. She almost regrets that she can't trust Rose. The two of them could relish this story over a glass of wine. But then it would be all over town.

"My kid could visit Lenore and me on the island in the summer. I could teach him to swim, and we could bike around the town. It would be great." Douglas has a notion he might be convincing Kyla of something.

"What does Lenore think of your great plan to save your marriage?"

"Well, she doesn't know about any of this. But she'd get used to it. She'd have to."

On the drive to the airport, Kyla falls into herself. She tries to disguise her inner silence with witty conversation and the recalling of shared anecdotes. She tries to erase the strange exchange with Douglas back at the house with memories of college and stories about the scenery. Despite her efforts, Douglas launches into a disjointed tirade about fatherhood in which the words *natural* and *unnatural* dominate. He is talking about fruits and seeds and immortality, while Kyla is trying to direct his attention to mango trees, to a cultivated achee, to the remnants of an orange grove dissected by the bypass from the highway. Suddenly, Douglas is talking about his own father, whom he calls the old man, making Kyla wonder if she is supposed to know him.

"The old man never understood me. He was always preoccupied with his damn job at that second-rate art school. He never had time for me, not for any of us. Now that he's retired, he hasn't changed. You think that when I went all the way home for a visit, he'd want to talk to his only son. No, he wants me to paint the fucking house."

Kyla is relieved to get to the airport parking lot, although it is a place where many bodies have been found in the trunks of many cars. She thinks the trip is over. She's only got to get him and his luggage out of the car. But Douglas grabs tight at the back of Kyla's honey hair and attempts to lock her eyes.

"You'd better not be lying to me about Donovan. There are tests, you know."

"Why would I lie to you?" Her blue eyes protrude.

"I guess you wouldn't. I'm sorry. It's just that this is a pretty passionate subject with me, and I just thought that maybe, well, that maybe. . . ."

Kyla pats his hand as he trails off. She knows that what he is suffering from is not passion, and she feels sorry for him. She decides to wait with him for his flight.

The baggage checked, they are absorbed in themselves, waiting for the time to pass in the late-night airport. Kyla is thinking about the idle threat of paternity tests. She wonders how much Douglas knows. She wonders if he knows that those blood tests could exclude a man as the possible father with ninety-nine percent accurate results. She wonders if he knows that it is pretty impossible to prove that any one man was the father of any one particular child. She wonders if he knows that even if the immunogenetic testing revealed that the HLA and RBC groups matched, and that there was a ninety-nine and one-half percent probability of paternity, it only meant that in a metropolitan area of one million males, there lived over four thousand possible fathers. Kyla loses herself in a reverie of numbers and statistics until she notices Douglas wiping his eyes with a soggy Kleenex.

She is flushed with a rush of pity for him. It must be awful to be a man, she thinks. To live in a body that can achieve conception but not experience it. Kyla is convinced that women can sense it. Every time she became pregnant, she immediately sat up on the edge of the bed feeling the tingling, the blooming.

It was such a useful signal. For then she took great pains to be alone for several weeks, to disappear mysteriously. She traveled to England the first time. She went to Canada the second time with a sixteen-month-old Rachel for company. The third and what she knew would be the last time, she took Rachel and Donovan to several communes in Montana, and then on to San Francisco. She made a point on each trip of meeting as many rugged and somewhat handsome blond men as possible. She wrote down their names, their approximate ages, and fudged the dates of these casual encounters in which usually not more than her travel plans or the weather were discussed. She kept this extensive list in her office. It was over a hundred times longer than the list in the secret place in her head. It could ultimately be reduced to a factor of seven, the number she had expelled from her favor, replacing it with four.

The boarding call. Douglas's eyes lean out of his sockets. He takes Kyla's large hand in his larger hands. His long finger traces the bones of her face.

"Let me ask you something personal, O.K.?" He waits for her slow nod. "Does the father know? I mean, Donovan's father. Or the girls' father? Does he know?"

"He doesn't care." Kyla's lie is the kind that relegates polygraphs to the realm of art rather than science, the kind of lie that can never be detected because the teller believes it absolutely.

"Well, tell him for me that he's a shit." And Douglas joins the line of other travelers laden with ski jackets as they prepare to leave a land where gigantic red-and-pink flowers fatten in the sun and the pale skin of children quickly toasts brown. Kyla watches him turn the corridor that leads into the jet. From the back, she thinks, he might be her father. She picks up the tissue Douglas left on his seat and stuffs it in the pocket of her too-tight jeans.

# LAKE HUDSON'S DAUGHTER

At least these two aren't always telling me how proud I should be of my mother; how brave she is; what a hero and inspiration and blah-blah-blah she is. These two are a little weird at times, but so were all the other women I've lived with in the past few years. The two Faiths in Indianapolis were probably the weirdest. It was really creepy the way each one kept repeating the other's name, which was, of course, her own name. I mean, Faith isn't all that common a name, and Indianapolis isn't all that small a town. I'd think they could each have found someone else.

The Faiths were creepiest at night. I'd be trying to sleep out in what was supposed to be a living room on some cushion they called a futon, but wasn't, and I could hear them in their bedroom. The first night I was there, I thought the cops were below their window. I was more naive then, and actually thought the FBI was tracking me. I could hear the Faiths yelling *police, police*. I didn't sleep all night, waiting for white men in blue suits to break down the door. I didn't relax until I heard the birds in the morning. My mother always got nervous at the first chirp of morning, but I like all noises that aren't made by people.

The next night I figured out they were yelling *please*. But the creepiest part was listening to each one crying and moaning and calling out her own name. I wondered if it was like making love to yourself.

In the morning, they'd act so polite, as if they had never touched each other. Maybe that was the weirdest part of all. I guess it was for my benefit, but I'm not a kid or anything. And I know all about lesbians. My mother's one, which is why I've been living in so many places lately.

One of the Faiths said I was privileged to not only be the daughter of a famous and fearless lesbian, but to have the opportunity to meet wonderful women across the country. I guess she thought that she and the other Faith were actually wonderful.

"It's like having lives in a lifetime," one Faith said.

"You're so lucky," the other Faith said.

"You're both stupid," I said.

I left not long after that. The Faiths said it was getting too hot, but I know they just got tired of me. I wondered where I would wake up next.

I've lived so many places and had so many different names, that it takes me at least an hour to wake up in the morning, even after I hear the birds. Most people wake up and think, what day is it? That way, if it's a school day or a work day, they can get depressed right away. I wake up and think, whose house am I in? What's my name supposed to be?

My mother's name never changes. She's Lake Hudson, as if she were a place and not a person. Visit the famous Lesbian Lawyer Lake! Only the lake is surrounded by bars: my mother is in jail in California, and I'm not allowed to visit her. Instead, I'm here in North Florida—or is it North Dakota?—with two lesbian lawyers, who are not famous and not named Lake.

Their names are Opal and Sonya. They call me Hadley, which is my real name. Most people just decide they will call me something else, although when I was with the witches in Wisconsin I got to pick out my own name. There was a ceremony and everything. I picked out Owl Wing. Everyone thought that was great. When I told them that my mother was petrified of owls, having once been swooped down on by one when she was a child, the witches called on the four winds to heal my mother of her fear. I started wondering whether she might not actually miss birds, being in prison and all. Anyway, I did get to wear feathers a lot.

My real name is Hadley Hudson. Hadley was the street where my father grew up: his family was known as the Hudsons of Hadley Street. Why my mother let me be named after a street sign, I'll never know, although that was before she was either a lesbian or a lawyer. She wasn't famous then either, except that she was married to a Hudson, my father, who everyone, except his mother, calls Hudson. I guess my mother liked him or his name or something enough to move away with him and change her own last name, of which she had already had several, courtesy of stepfathers. Grandmother Hudson once said my mother was a bastard, and always said at least my mother's name wasn't *River*, but I never understood that until last year when I lived in New York with the lesbian theater troupe.

I guess my mother even liked him enough to have *me*, though she told me that she had thought long and hard about getting one of those newly legal abortions when she found out she was pregnant. She said she assumed I'd change her life. I have. I've made her famous.

My mother is a cause célèbre, at least that's what the articles say. I came across an old one in the bathroom. Opal and Sonya must have been reading up on the case before I got here. I sat on the toilet and read the article, probably for the fiftieth time. And for probably the fiftieth time I got mad. All those words about how *she* suffers, how *she* is noble and wonderful and full of integrity, how *she* is a victim of patriarchy and injustice and heterosexism. Not a single word about me. Not one word. It pisses the shit out of me.

I don't even feel guilty about getting angry anymore. I was cured of guilt out at Featherstone Feminist Farm, more than a year ago, when I became the youngest member of the anarcho/lesbo/seperato collective. No one asked me whether I wanted to be a member of the collective, or even if I felt anarcho or lesbo, although I certainly felt seperato. I even felt seperato from Terry, who probably thought I had a crush on her because I followed her around so much. I just thought she was so sensible. Unlike most of the other women there, unlike my mother. Terry was a therapist, like most of the women there. Unlike my mother. My father, a psychiatrist, always said that therapists were the bastards of the field. My mother would nod in agreement, like she always did before she became a lesbian lawyer.

It was Terry who took me to town to telephone my father. I called him at his office after hours, and he answered the phone. He sounded less fierce than I remembered. I think my mother was always a little afraid of him. When I heard his voice, I hung up. I didn't have anything to say.

Terry and the other anarcho/lesbo/seperatos taught me that guilt is silly. Every morning at the farm, before breakfast even, we each picked out our feeling for the day. It was important to name our feelings, Terry always said. There were two blackboards, one with *O.K.* and one with *Could Be Better.* Guilt was definitely *Could Be Better,* along with fear and greed and envy. So every morning I picked out my feeling for that day—grumpy, which was on the *O.K.* blackboard. Terry always picked out peaceful which was also on the *O.K.* blackboard. I got very good at being grumpy, but I guess Terry was not so good at being peaceful. She left the farm to do relief work in Jordan.

I'm still pretty good at being grumpy, but grumpy is a lot like angry. It makes me feel stupid. Stupid and impatient. Impatient to be eighteen and free and an adult. I'm tired of being only a daughter.

Meanwhile, I'm here in wherever-I-am, living with whoever-they-are and their kid, Powell. When I first saw the kid, I thought I'd been enlisted as the free babysitter, but it hasn't been like that, at least so far. Powell is really not bad for a seven-year-old boy. It's been awhile since I've been around boys, so it's kind of fun. Especially since I never have to watch him, and I don't even have to share a room with him.

I haven't had my own room since I lived with both my parents. This room is not as nice, of course: it doesn't have wallpaper with a geometric design or sliding mirrored-closet doors, but it is just as big. Best of all, I've got my own windows. They face west, into a pasture. Opal said we could buy curtains for my room if I wanted, but I don't want to. I like to come home from school and watch the sun set behind the cows, the cattle egrets sucking bugs from between hooves and never getting stepped on.

Sonya told me that cattle egrets aren't even natives. She said they've only been here from Africa since the fifties, though they've multiplied like crazy and now there are more of them than the regular egrets that have been around here forever. Sonya knows lots of neat things like that. Sometimes after school she'll be home, and she'll walk me out into that pasture. In the late winter afternoon, it feels as cold as North Dakota. I like wearing Opal's wool coat, even if it is plaid. Sonya lets me look close up at the furry-eared cows and snow-white birds.

It's strange being in school again. The third day I was here, Opal said I was going to school. I was certainly surprised. I mean, I'm a fugitive, and who ever heard of a fugitive going to junior high. Besides, I thought I could just stay at the house and read. I told Sonya that.

"Read what?" she said.

I thought this was a crazy question. These women had a whole roomful of books. The room didn't have any heat, but I guess that kept the books better.

"Anything," I answered.

Then I told her what I'd ben reading. I told her that I'd read Mary Daly at the Faiths', Judy Grahn near the Hudson River, Audre Lorde at Featherstone, and Starhawk with the witches in Wisconsin. I didn't mention all the Naiad novels I'd read looking for the sex scenes, or *On Our Backs*.

"Forget it," Sonya said.

"But I don't need to go to school," I said.

"Need has nothing to do with it," Opal said. "Need it or not, you're going to school."

"Why?" I challenged. I saw Powell watching closely.

"It's the law, for one thing," Sonya said. She smiled slightly. I thought I saw a dimple, but it was gone very quickly.

"You want to keep your first name, right," Opal stated more than asked. "But you'll need a different last one so that we can say you are our sister. Pick a name—Rugerrio or Overstreet."

"Overstreet," I said. I kind of liked Rugerrio better, but I thought Overstreet was funnier. The Hudsons of Overstreet.

"Fine," Opal said, but I thought she sounded disappointed. I tried not to feel guilty. Even though I learned guilt was not O.K. at Featherstone, I also learned a lot about racism and classism and elitism. I didn't want to be insensitive about Opal's last name, which sounded foreign to me. I didn't want to be accused of being a privileged Anglo twit, like I was when I stayed with the lesbian theater troupe in New York. It was true, I was white and privileged. But then again, most of the women I'd been meeting seemed to be.

I apologized to Opal.

"Hadley," she said, "just relax."

Sonya said that I'd probably read too many issues of *off our backs*. I didn't tell her that I did read every issue, looking for mention of Lake Hudson, the place if not the person.

"I'll get the birth certificate and all tomorrow," Sonya said.

"Mine?" I was a bit surprised.

"No. Hadley Overstreet's. School records for this good student, a recent transfer from a large school district."

"Isn't that illegal?" I asked.

"Of course," they both said.

They sure are strange lawyers. Not just because they make me go to school because it's the law and then break the law to get me in, but other things, too. Like their office. It doesn't even have any carpeting. It's about a mile from this old farmhouse we live in, and still out in the middle of nowhere.

The way they dress is another thing: jeans, like they are going to take a hike out in the pasture. They don't wear stockings or suits unless one of them has to go to a hearing or trial. Then one of them practically has to dress the other one who is cursing up and down.

My mother always wore silk suits and sheer stockings to work on the fourteenth floor of the Kruger Building. She had an eel skin briefcase that Grandmother Hudson gave her when she graduated law school and a diamond watch that Hudson had given her for the same thing. I guess Hudson and his mother didn't know that being a lawyer would make my mother a lesbian.

My mother met Paige at the firm. Paige is my mother's lover, another lesbian lawyer, but more like my mother than like Opal or Sonya. Paige's father had been Hudson's attorney. Hudson wasn't too happy to find out about my mother and Paige. He started screaming about how divorce wouldn't be good enough for my mother, and about how at least Paige's father wasn't alive to see his daughter turned into a dyke. That was the first time I heard the word *dyke*, though it wasn't the last, and certainly not the last time I heard the word *divorce*.

It wasn't the first time I'd heard about divorce. In grade school, I'd sit up in my bed in the room with the geometric wallpaper, watching myself in the mirrored closet doors and listen to them argue. My father, the psychiatrist, would say my mother was low rent and had married him for his money. My mother, the law student, would say my father was a pig and had married her for her body. One of them would mention divorce. The other would mention me. I'd start to worry about something I'd spilled at dinner. If I kept on being bad, no one would want me.

Then I'd hear ugly sounds coming from their bedroom, somewhere between laughs and cries. I'd hear my father call, *Jesus, Jesus,* as if that were my mother's name. Then it would get real quiet, so quiet I could hear the water running my parents' bathroom.

At breakfast, they would smile and kiss each other, like nothing had happened. Even though I was a kid, I knew. I tried to be polite. But then I would spill something or say something stupid and I could feel them start to get mad at each other again.

When Powell spills something, no one yells. Though Sonya gets mad when Powell squishes spaghetti through his teeth.

"Stop it," she yells.

Opal laughs. "Didn't you do that when you were a kid, oh my perfect baby dyke?"

"That's different," Sonya says, trying to be grumpy. I could give her a few lessons.

"Are you trying to say we eat too much spaghetti? Are you maligning my ethnic heritage?"

"Fuck your heritage," Sonya says. "We do eat too much spaghetti. And too much broccoli."

The next Saturday we drive to Georgia.

"Do you like barbecue?" Opal says.

"I thought we were vegetarians," I say.

"We are," Opal says. "Very strict. And that's why we're going to Georgia."

"If it happens in Georgia, it doesn't count," Sonya explains.

The ribs are greasy and good. It's all-you-can-eat night. Powell and I split another plate. It's been a long time since I've eaten meat. I listen to Sonya and Opal talk about law stuff.

"I think there's got to be a responsive pleading," Opal says.

"Oh shit," Sonya says. "Does that mean we're screwed for attorney's fees again?"

"Afraid so."

"More ribs?" Sonya laughs.

I laugh too. I'd told Sonya and Opal about one dinner with the witches in Wisconsin. They were very strict vegetarians, no butter or anything. I couldn't imagine them ever eating barbecue, no matter where they were. It was pretty boring to eat with them. And the dinner conversation was pretty boring, too. They were always talking about unity and telepathy. So, one night Raven says to me, "Owl Wing, would you like some more tabouli?" And I say, "Raven, what kind of witch are you that you don't already know?" No one laughed then, but Sonya and Opal seem to think it's pretty funny.

"Those damned landlords will eventually win. Maybe we should put a hex on them," Sonya says, still sort of laughing.

"There should be a hex for attorney's fees."

"Or at least a damn statute."

"The law sure is fucked up." I say this, although I hadn't really meant to. I was just thinking it, and suddenly my mouth was moving.

Sonya nods. If I was at Featherstone Farm right now, someone would be asking me to express my feelings, but Sonya just keeps nodding. Then she says, "Sure is."

I'm a little embarrassed. I hate for people to feel sorry for me. So, the law is fucked up. Everyone knows that. But people use *me* to prove that it is; or at least use my famous lesbian lawyer mother, Lake, as an example. Lake Hudson is sitting in a jail in California as I eat ribs in Georgia because she won't tell the court where I am. I wonder if she even knows where I am anymore. I wonder if I even want her to know where I am anymore. I like living with Sonya and Opal and Powell. I even like school.

But if my mother tells the court where I am, she gets out of jail. It's the same court that told my mother that my father gets custody of me because she's a lesbian. I guess she doesn't like that court very much.

I guess I don't either.

Everybody is real quiet on the way back to Florida. Powell falls asleep in the backseat, leaning on me, but I don't mind all that much. When we get home, I go sit on my bed and look out the curtainless window. I can hear Powell yelling in the yard.

Opal runs into my room. "Come outside, quick!"

Our front yard is filled with birds, all screeching and flying this way and that and pecking at the ground. They swoop down at the cats, who run for cover under the house.

"What are they?" Opal asks Sonya.

"Blackbirds, it looks like. Or maybe grackles."

Whatever they are, there seem to be millions of them. I can't even see the ground.

"My mother is terrified of birds," I say. Then, as if the birds have heard me and been insulted, there's a terrible screaming as the whole flock starts flapping and rising. The east sky blackens with wings like a really bad bruise.

"That sounds sensible to me," Sonya says.

We all go inside.

# POVERTY:
# A
# STORY

It is extremely breezy and slightly eerie and the talk is of hurricanes. The clerks in Blessings Market are crossing the windows with cut-rate masking tape until several huge manila-colored union jacks appear. Customers line up at the check-out counter with baskets full of canned beans and canned peaches.

Across the road, the workers from Street Legal Services pack the reception area of their storefront office with their jabbing voices and pressing laughter. The younger secretary leans against the door. The huge windows of Street Legal Services remain unprotected as the rain slants into the glass. The three lawyers do not have umbrellas. The two secretaries do. The paralegal thinks hers is in her car. All the clients are somewhere else, some safely sheltered, others not. The street is empty.

The six legal services workers look posed, as if for an affirmative action poster. There is only one man among them; he is half-Japanese and wholly gay. There are two Anglo women, two Black women, and one Hispanic woman. One of the women is over sixty. Two of the women are unwed mothers. Three of the women have been divorced at least once. Most of the workers grew up poor. All of the bodies crowding the reception room at Street Legal Services have survived at least one hurricane.

One of the workers once wanted to be a writer. I have even taken courses in creative writing and have studied great works of fiction. I was serious, oh so serious, about craft, and thought that one could learn to craft a story in the same way one could learn to craft a potholder. Different colors, different patterns, but generally the same size and shape. Still, it could be a romantic profession. I imagined myself living in a garret and writing lengthy convoluted novels.

I do, in fact, live in a modified garret but I don't have much time to devote to a magnum opus. My only chance to write is when I'm not working or recovering from working, which isn't very often. It's a real pity I need sleep.

I'm also not as interested in craft as I once was. If I still believed its dictates, I couldn't write this story, for I've learned that one should never shift points of view within a short story. My teachers would not accept me as narrator of this story as well as one of the third-person characters within it. They would also not accept the number of characters I've included, for a short story should only have one or two major and very well defined characters. But poverty is crowded, and this may not be a short story at all.

On the bulletin board of Street Legal Services are statistics published by various organizations: *Nine Million Americans Live in Chronic Poverty; 36% of All Blacks Are Poor; Two Out of Every Three Adults in Poverty Are Women.* There are graphs, charts, geographical rosters, and columns of decimal points below each of these bold-faced facts. The legal services workers recognize that facts are different from realities. Facts are supported by numbers.

The workers do not believe in numbers. They know that the government tries to reduce the number of poor people by changing a few definitions. The poverty line is as thick and as imaginary as the equator. It is, however, much harder to cross the line going north than to slip south. The hallway bulletin board proclaims that there has been a continuous rise in the number of people living below the poverty line, despite the government's best efforts at statistical gerrymandering. There are more graphs and decimal points which attest to this truth.

For the workers, the only facts are the clients. The day before the hurricane warning, the paralegal interviewed seventeen clients. Fourteen of them had been denied social security disability benefits because government doctors had determined these people were able to work. One was a woman who had to use her teeth to open her purse. Another was a man who had no teeth; his withered arm jerked wildly as he asked to have everything repeated three times. None of these clients had more than a seventh-grade education. The government had determined that each could do sedentary work, like clerical or perhaps secretarial. Two of the clients could not sign their names.

The newest attorney is still unsettled by people who cannot read or write. She sometimes forgets that her own grandparents are illiterate. She sometimes wonders why she works in legal services at all, it depresses her so. She certainly doesn't do it for the money. All the workers could triple their salaries if they worked in private practice. For the attorneys, this means they could be making sixty or seventy thousand dollars a year. Sometimes it is convenient not to believe in numbers.

Yet the workers often feel extraordinarily fortunate. One of the unwed mothers was driving home late from work, about a week before the hurricane warning, when two of her bald tires blew out. Of course, she had no money and only one spare. But she did have a credit card. She is not poor. There are differences between being broke, even incessantly broke, and being poor. She wonders if her child will be able to appreciate such distinctions.

The attorneys who grew up poor learned these distinctions from the glints of the broken bathroom windows of their respective childhoods, thousands of miles apart. They were schooled by the cracked vinyl of their mothers' shoes, by their guidance counselors' assumptions in pigeon-holing them for vocational training despite their excellent grades, by their own gray socks and segregated schools. They are told, now, that they are American dreams; that they pulled themselves up by their own bootstraps. They are told to say anyone can do it, but they never say that. They, unlike some of the few who escaped poverty and went into politics, do not believe their own reprieve should be attributed solely to their drive and ambition. They believe that life is arbitrary and cruel; that life steps all over you with its expensive shoes when you least expect it. They believe they have been lucky—at least so far.

Luck is not even the half of it, as the woman over sixty will tell you. She has been here for ten years, having resurrected herself from several deaths in different cities. She is almost happy here, with her new work, her new life.

Do you know where *here* is? A good short story should set the scene quickly and accurately. That's the purpose of sentences like, "The scent of dogwoods wafted through the Peachtree Street air." From reading that, you should be able to surmise that it's spring in Atlanta.

I'm not such a clever writer, however. There are only two seasons in this place, and one of them is hurricane season. Of course, the hurricane should be a clue that this is near a coast, probably in the South. But a writer always has to rely on the reader. What if you don't know anything about hurricanes? The union jack may have confused you, made you think of England. Perhaps I've gotten you wandering around Australia with all that stuff about being south of the equator. I apologize if I misled you out of the United States, the richest nation in the world. I probably should have been blunt right from the beginning: Blessings Market is in Palm Beach County, Florida.

You see why I wasn't forthright. Palm Beach conjures up visions of white sand, palm trees, polo games, and mansions. The Rockefellers, the Roosevelts, the Kennedys all winter here. In today's newspaper, you can read that Yoko Ono is putting the El Salano mansion on the market for a mere eight million dollars. Now that John Lennon is dead, twenty rooms *do* seem a bit excessive for a widow and her growing boy.

The boys and girls of poorer women grow up west of El Salano. West Palm Beach is a city some think exists solely to house maids and chauffeurs and propagate future maids and chauffeurs. There are also towns with rather romantic sounding names like Delray Beach, Riviera Beach, and Boynton Beach, with sizable poor populations insulated from the new condominiums rising from every available scrap of land. Further west, through the desolate glades into the fertile black soil surrounding Lake Okeechobee, is the city of Belle Glade, dense with dark families living ten to a room meant for one. It could be confused with an underdeveloped nation in Central America. Even the sickening smell of the sweet corporate profits of sugar cane pollutes the air. But Belle Glade, as they say, is another story.

As for this story, it is still raining. One could call it torrential. One of the legal services workers does.

"What a torrential downpour," a Black woman says.

"Just like in Asia. What are those terrific rains in India?" the Hispanic woman asks.

"Monsoon," the half-Japanese man offers.

"It sure is crazy out there. Shit," one of the Anglo women mutters, shaking her head.

"Do you think I should leave?" I finally ask.

"Don't know, it's raining pretty hard. The road looks flooded."

"No. Not today. I mean *leave*. Leave for good."

"For good? Do you have another job?"

"No, not really. I thought I'd write."

"How you going to eat?"

"I thought I'd get food stamps."

"Hey, they don't taste so good."

We all laugh at our stale, soggy joke. No one is shocked that I want to leave. We all talk about leaving from time to time. Our jobs have high turnover rates to match the high frustration factor. Long hours. Bad pay. Few rewards.

Yet this particular assortment of workers has been at this particular storefront of Street Legal Services for several years. They are with each other more than they are with anyone else. They do everything together except sleep, though they have been known to even do that if the night is late and drunk enough. They consider themselves a collective, much to the consternation of the administrative office, which believes, like the Politburo, in the sanctity of centralization.

"It's really pouring. We need a radio. Where's our radio?" the younger secretary asks.

"Antonio took it two years ago when he left," the secretary who is not the younger one answers.

"It was his, wasn't it?" one of the attorneys asks.

"Of course," another attorney answers.

Then everyone turns to the newest attorney to describe the circumstances of Antonio's departure, anecdotes which the newest attorney has heard so many times that they seem to describe events experienced rather than related second hand. The workers describe cleaning out Antonio's office after he left and finding pairs of everything: two staplers, two tape dispensers, two dictating machines (one broken), and two two-hole punches. They talk about his last weeks of work when he was higher than usual, arrived later than usual, and departed even earlier, so that his total time in the office dwindled to about thirty-five minutes a day. They recollect his clients, lining up with their deportation papers, waiting for Antonio to save their lives and prevent their exile to certain death in Guatemala, El Salvador, Chile, Nicaragua. Sometimes Antonio even won their cases.

The strangest thing about Antonio, the newest attorney had once thought, was that despite the rancor of the complaints about him, he seemed to have been genuinely liked.

"He *was* a lot of fun," one or the other of his former coworkers would laugh.

But no one misses him. When you leave a group you've become a part of, a hole grows in the place your voice occupied. Then the vines of other voices root in the hole and cover it over, their greens sometimes strikingly like the missing green, sometimes unique. You become the tale told rather than the teller. You become compost.

"The rain is thick as shit out there." One of the unwed mothers says this.

"Perhaps you could take a vacation," one of the divorcees suggests to the would-be writer. "Instead of quitting, just take some time off for some peace and quiet, to unwind and write." She sees writing as a relaxing hobby, like fishing.

"You already go to writing conferences once in a while," the man adds, as if conferences provided time to write.

The workers try to peer across the street. They can no longer see the masking-tape union jacks on the windows of Blessings Market. The office lights flick off and instantly return to their normally dingy fluorescence. Then, again.

The wind and rain suddenly stop, but the lights keep flicking. Street Legal Services is in the eye of a blinking hurricane. In the still- ness, the workers can hear water running. The roof is leaking. Again.

Rivulets of water make patterns on the walls, illuminated for a moment, then dark. The world looks yellow. The phones do not ring. It has never been so quiet.

The last writing conference I went to was three years ago and was called OOPS, the Organization of Poetic Scholars. When I en- rolled, I thought they were joking. It was a rather serious, self-important affair, however, threatening to become an annual bash of writers proclaiming they were neither serious nor self-important. Someone suggested that each year the name of the gathering could be changed, provided it always have the same acronym. Some people can only tolerate creativity if it produces a desired predestined result. Sugges- tions abounded. One man proposed we describe ourselves as Ostra- cized, Outre, and Poverty-Stricken. OOPS.

I rankled. I'd like to blame the half-glass of cheap wine for what therapists might term my inappropriate response. I screamed.

"Poverty? You don't know what *poverty* is!" I was thinking of the man's tenured professorship, his gentrified and restored house, his leather briefcase. Most of all, I admit, I was coveting his powder blue Volvo.

"And you do?" It was a question and a challenge. This speaker was another man, stereotypically sensitive and sporting a very sin- cere beard. He'd already told every woman at the conference that he believed in something he called gender justice. The only discernible difference between him and the man with the Volvo was tenure track as opposed to tenure. I decided this wasn't enough of a difference to make a difference. I also decided to treat his statement as an invi- tation to introduce an accurate but sufficiently literary definition of poverty, which I was quickly trying to formulate.

"Poverty is when you have to use your teeth to open your purse— but why bother? There's nothing in it but an expired Medicaid card and the address of the Salvation Army shelter."

That wasn't as witty as I'd hoped. No one laughed, or said any- thing at all. I felt myself becoming a character, a piece of dialogue in someone else's story, the punch line of a joke. My face flushed until the talk turned to other things, although it never did turn to my second favorite subject, hurricanes.

The paralegal thinks the floor under her feet is getting wet. She takes off her shoe and rubs her toes along the tile. It is. Water seeps in the door. The glass whistles, louder and louder.

Suddenly it is like waking up under a full-blast shower with your party clothes still on. Have you gotten drunk or what happened? The roof seems like it has collapsed, but the plaster is only torn as if it were a piece of the cheap yellow paper the attorneys use to draft their pleadings. The sound of water deafens any attempt at conversation. The bulletin board bangs down from the wall, hardly heard. Flyers describing food stamp eligibility requirements zoom around the room in small irregular circles, until their income guidelines become soggy and heavy and sink to the fast-forming puddles on the dirty gray floor.

I must end this story now, for we are being evacuated. A good short story should leave the reader wanting more. That is something I never learned from studying craft or at any conference. I made it up myself.

Some readers will protest that this piece does not fulfill its promise. For a story entitled "Poverty," not much of the plot revolves around being poor. There isn't much of a plot, either. In fact, you might not think it should be correctly labeled a story.

Them's the breaks, as they say. Besides, I've decided I'm staying with Street Legal Services, come hell or high water, or both. With a day job, I can afford to flaunt literary conventions. As for other conventions, being unconventional is virtually part of the job description at Street Legal Services.

When the hurricane is just another story told in the storefront across the street from Blessings Market, the workers will still be gathering in the reception area. The sun will be seduced by the new windows and will unveil its rays in the narrow spaces between the clustered people. A few clients will be sitting inside, those who can't read or who need to have everything repeated three times.

One afternoon it will start to rain, and the people in the reception area will be stranded without umbrellas. They will know it is just an afternoon shower and they need only wait. To pass the time, the Street Legal Services worker who is taking an acting class will read a piece aloud from a new little magazine. The small crowd in the room will understand why it is a story; that it is about poverty.

# THE FLOOR

not exactly the old-fashioned way: i use paper towels.

but still, down on my hands and knees. i never learned to use a
mop. or maybe i can't see well enough to use one. at least, that's
what i tell myself as i'm here with the ammonia fumes stretching
my nostrils and doing who the hell knows what to my brain;
as i'm here with the sweat congealing around my plastic glasses;
as i'm here using my barely over-the-tip-of-flesh fingernails as a
scrub brush to scratch off a spot of red something.

blood red something. probably a tomato squished under my heel.
(i've been trying to eat more salads. since i can't pay money to
exercise, i try to compensate.)
or some strawberry jelly from one of the kid's lunch sandwiches.
(how i hate to fill those sesame street thermoses at seven in the
morning. and remember whether it's big bird or bert & ernie
that gets apple juice and not chocolate milk.)
or some sauce from the pizza my most recently former lover
brought when she wasn't my former lover.

(has it really been that long since i've scrubbed this damn place?)

"this white kitchen floor is the bane of my existence." i say that to
no one in particular, because no one in particular is here,
except the dog, who doesn't answer. we've been together since he was
six-weeks old. and now he's almost sixteen.
the kids are asleep, as they should be at two in the morning. i like
to say sentences with words like *bane* in them as i wash the floor.
a little drama is good for the soul. and since i avoid drama in my
life at all costs (just ask any one of my former lovers), i have to get
my quota somehow.

but under my breath, i curse my mother (who else?). she schooled
me in the unfulfillable desire for eternal cleanliness. she gave me the
gift of guilt which enables me to be on my knees in the middle of
the night without reference to the erotic.

suffering from an attack of fairness, i curse the door. if the door did
its job, i wouldn't be here. that door can't keep the dog and kids inside
and can't keep the damp, sandy clay outside.

i wipe up another partial footprint, animal or sneaker. or perhaps
both, one embossed over the other.

and then another red spot.
small and circular.

in the midst of another fairness attack—wondering why i can't have
an anxiety attack like one of my former lovers—i decide that it's not
really the door's fault.
and i can never sustain my mother-blaming for very long.
we have to eat.
it must be a piece of watermelon flesh. or sauce from last week's ziti.
if only i could blame a former lover, that would solve everything. but
my favorite lover is a former lover: their faults are more easily forgiven,
and i don't have to wake up next to them.

i corner myself to the edge of the kitchen. near the trash can full of paper towels. done!

but i should have made myself a cup of coffee. or gotten a can of diet coke, but not the caffeine-free kind. i mean, why drink it if it doesn't have caffeine?
a real insomniac doesn't need stimulants. i take a small comfort in this. i like comforts, even small ones.

and i like the privacy of night.
and i like to read.
something good. certainly not the monthly reports i brought home from work like i'm important or something. that's what the aforementioned-most-recently-former-lover once said: "you think you're hot shit because you manage the vine street 7-eleven." i mean, besides pointing out it wouldn't be really flattering to be shit, hot or otherwise, what could i say? i try to remember whether this was before the pizza or after.

no, something good. not the book on lesbian mothers. or the one on mothers of lesbians. i don't want to read about myself tonight. or my kids. or my mother.
no, i want to read something steamy.

cassady moans.

cassady is the dog. he follows me to the bookshelf in my bedroom. i like my bedroom. a lot. it's the reason i rented this house, selfish to admit. the wide windows. the double closet. but especially the rosebud pink carpeting. i mean, most rental places have brown or avocado or a kind of vomity gold. this was a real find.
but now i find a dark stain next to my bed. it looks like a rorschach blot intended to elicit responses regarding women: stuff like *circle, womb, moon, egg, fist.*

i push my glasses to the bridge of my nose with my index finger, as if this will make me see better.

in the morning, i am going to kill those kids with their kool-aid, magic

markers, whatevers.
the novel i found didn't suit my moods.
the dog mirrors my restlessness.
i hear sleep-talking from the children's beds.

the younger one wakes up, wanting something to drink.
the other one wakes up wanting to be included.
we pad toward the kitchen. i hope the floor is dry.
"hold the damn dog back," i say, "while i get you some chocolate milk."

"i want apple juice," is the one answer.
the other answer is a one-eyed nod.
neither answer is sufficient to keep the dog back.
how can i complain? the dog weighs more than both of them put
together.
luckily the floor is dry.

the kids fall asleep at the table.
it is almost time to get them up.
i put them in their beds for that all-important dawn sleep.
i make myself some coffee. caffeinated, of course.

under the table is another red spot. shit, i say, wondering if i missed
something.
i put my finger on it.
it is wet. fresh. not crusted with ammonia.
i put my finger to my nose.
i have never been too good with the sense of smell.
i put my finger to my tongue.
after all, mom, my floors are clean enough to eat off.

blood. definitely blood.

my hand goes to my crotch. i haven't felt it dripping. but sometimes
menstruation doesn't bother to issue me a timely invitation.

i am dry. real dry.
i weave my finger around my running shorts into myself.

i am dry. dry as that book i was trying to read.

i go to the kids. i inspect them for cuts. for wounds. their flesh is unsevered.

the dog?

when i was a kid we had a female dog. i never call dogs bitches, i think that's ugly. she would get her period and slide around the blue linoleum of my mother's kitchen and bedroom. my mother would put a piece of cardboard across the door to the parlor, where my sisters and i slept on mattresses flopped on the thin aqua carpeting. the dog couldn't pass the threshold. she was a very small dog.

the dog cassady is in the kitchen. he is male. i didn't want a male, but he was so cute as a puppy. all furry and sweet. and the female of the litter was taken. or so i was told by a lover whose full name i no longer care to remember.

i run my hands through cassady's fur. this takes a while, he's got a lot of it. i sometimes think he would weigh much less if i had him clipped. he looks so skinny when he's had a bath. kind of like an undernourished great dane. he's supposed to be half dane, but father-hood is fictional at best. or so i tell my children, giving them a pre-view of my rehearsed facts-of-life speech.

his mother was a saint bernard. how can you go wrong with a dog named after a saint, i reasoned, even a male saint.

the dog's fine.

i roll him on his back to check. he's fine.

i scratch near the nub of his tail. he's bleeding.

a small spurt, an ooze really, from his penis.

i can't believe this. i look again.

a miniature puddle forms on the floor.

oh shit.

blood red blood.

i wipe it up with a piece of paper towel.

i continue to wipe up that spot all day: while i make lunches for the
kids; while i drop them off at day care; while i pencil my monthlies
at the 7-eleven; while i check in the delivery of chocolate milk from
the guy who always leers at me; while i take a break to again figure
out how i can afford to get the dog to the vet; while i watch the part-
timer mop the floor in slow motion as i wait on the lunchtime crowd;
while i get off and pick up the kids again and drive home listening
to them fight and open the door expecting to find my home crowded
with spots of red all bleeding into each other until the floor is an
amoeba that will swallow us whole.

the door opens on a room with a redless floor. it is as clean as we
left it. and quieter.

the dog does not greet us. i call his name. the children call his name.

i used to think cassady was a strange name for a dog, but over a
decade and a half of overuse has cured me of such a notion. my then
lover (what *was* her name?) insisted on cassady. she thought she was
jack kerouac, and she named the dog in hopes he would be the kind
of companion i wasn't. i tried to convince her to at least compromise
on cody, which is the first name of kerouac's buddy in novels other
than *on the road*. cody, i thought, i could live with, especially if i tied
a red bandana around the puppy's neck. but she was a real anglophile
(from barbados) and thought it was very sheik to use last names as
first names. something about the island's upper classes. (i never asked
which island.) crazy to realize now, but i gave both the kids last names
as first.

i thought it would deflect attention from their last names.
i thought it would prevent confusion.
but their names sound amazingly like cassady.
and i become confused whenever i need to yell at only one of them.

the children have never known a time cassady has not come to the
door when they came home, except for the time the wind (i guess)
had slammed the bathroom door shut while he was in there (probably
drinking out of the toilet), and he was trapped in that tiny place (for
who knows how long) not even howling.

i rush the kids to their room. look under their beds. no dog among
the dust bunnies. close the door. "play with the toys in your closet."

it doesn't take long to find such a huge dog in a small house. he's
under the kitchen table.

there's no blood.
i squat beside him. i put my hand to his mouth, but he doesn't lick
it. his nose is hard and warm. he doesn't seem to be breathing.

i decide to call someone—not my mother.
i have an address book full of women i've left, always telling them
the same thing:
"honey/dear/babe/love/whatever"
(but never their names)
"it isn't you—it's just that i'm incapable of commitment."
if she mentions the dog, i say i'm incapable of commitment to humans.
if she mentions the dog and the kids, i say i'm incapable of commitment
to adult humans.

i decide to telephone my most recently former lover, but only because
i can still remember her phone number without looking it up.

she promises to come right over.
she is not only good in emergencies, she loves them.

"he has a pulse," she tells me.

"of course, he does," i answer.

she hefts the dog into the back of her car.
"wait here," she tells me.
"where would i go?" i ask.

i should have gone with her, i say an hour later. two hours later.

i lift the telephone receiver. i don't call my mother. i don't replace
the receiver until the recording commands me to hang up. i lift the
telephone receiver again. i don't call my mother.

i feed the kids bread and butter and coffee for dinner. no one
complains.

i decide to quit my job. i've been there almost six months. i will quit
it the way i quit lovers: with proper notice and silence.
"tell me what's wrong so that we can work it out," bosses and soon-
to-be former lovers say to me. but i never can explain.
i've already quit more jobs than the IRS calculates that three people
will have in a lifetime
(or so they told me in a telephone audit).
i've left more lovers than the average sexually active person with have
in a lifetime
(or so i read in a bestseller we sell at the 7-eleven).

my most recently former lover comes back without the dog.

"they had to put him to sleep," she says.

i don't ask who *they* were. i don't ask anything. what could a question
do?

"your phone was busy," she says.
she sounds jealous.

"i tried to call you," she says.
she sounds suitably annoyed.

"i thought you'd rather me take care of everything," she says.
i don't know whether that is true or not.

"he was an old dog," she says.
i know that better than anyone. about thirty times as old as our affair.
more than three times older than my oldest child. older than the days
when i was a witch and he was my familiar. old enough to witness
my first gay pride march.

"say something," she says.

"that dog is my longest-lasting relationship—except for my mother."
i used to say it as a joke.
or as a small comfort to lovers who were soon to be former: letting
them believe all responsibilities were mine.
i had said it to her, hadn't i?

my former lover is trying to maintain her kindness, but the crisis is
over. she is winding down, as if from a drug. i am honest when i say
i don't mind if she leaves. it's late. i have to get the kids to sleep.

she offers to stay over, to spend the night.
i shake my head.
she laughs.
she calls me a bitch and says i'll never change.

the kids can't sleep. they don't know what sleep means anymore. "why
did they want cassady to sleep? and where's he sleeping, now?" the
older one asks.
i wonder whether i should say something about heaven.
they're scared to death of death.
or maybe it's the coffee.

i scoop them up into bed with me. one on each side. i hope it comforts
them as much as it does me.

i fall asleep, i guess. it's a blankness. my grief is too new to give me dreams.

when i wake, the kids are lightly snoring. i turn them on their sides and they stop. but i still can't go back to sleep. i slither out the bottom of the bed from in between their soft-smelling bodies.

i collide with the bookshelf and scrape my knee.

i find my glasses. i guess i'll make coffee.

in the kitchen, i want to call my mother. i try to figure out if it's too late (or too early) in her time zone. if it's two a.m. here. . .

i am still making calculations as i pour from the pitcher of cherry kool-aid;
as i dump ragu meatless spaghetti sauce from a saucepan;
as i spill sweet-and-sour sauce, raspberry yogurt, maraschino cherries;
as i start to smash economy-size jars of strawberry jelly
and then i am on my hands and knees,
scrubbing every red thing into the whiteness of the floor, without a paper towel.

# THE
# POOL

It is never clean enough for her. There is always at least a splayed leaf floating until it becomes saturated and sinks to the bottom like a shadow without an object. Sometimes there is an insect, a dragonfly with its wet wings furiously beating, its life dependent on flight; or a yellow-jacket with its stripes fading into a pale blue. Once there was a frog, bloated with death. She ignored it until Tina came home, and after dinner, sitting on the concrete deck in the twilight drinking Kahlua and coffee, she casually pointed it out to Tina, as if she had just then noticed it. Tina, predictably and stoically, got the net and fished out the stiff amphibian. Tina deposited the animal in the tall grass which leaned against the wall that surrounded the pool which Tina never used. Tina, freckled white, did not even like to sunbathe near the pool's reflective glare. She burnt easily.

Augusta, Tina's lover, had beige flesh that tanned slowly but successfully. Augusta swam. Augusta spent her daylight summer hours studying the water in the pool or the absence of reflections on the gray wall. The wall did not seem tall enough to Augusta. It was the legal limit, according to Tina, but Augusta wondered what a therapist knew about the law. Augusta thought that perhaps they should break glass bottles, preferably thick liquor bottles, into sharp pieces and cement them to the top of the wall. Augusta had seen this in Mexico, and even then she had thought it attractively useful. Tina disapproved of the idea. Augusta idly plotted its execution.

Even with the frog gone, the pool reminds Augusta of a fouled pond. She complains to Tina, who does not answer. Annoyed, Augusta retreats and pours the remains of her cold coffee and Kahlua into the kitchen sink. She goes to bed without Tina. Augusta later listens to Tina's familiar voice modulate with the intimacy of conversation. Tina must be on the phone to her newest, Augusta thinks, almost without rancor, as she falls asleep.

In the morning, after Tina is gone, Augusta telephones the pool company.

It is still morning when Augusta and the pool woman find themselves—and each other—on the kitchen floor, a few steps from the tinted sliding glass doors which separate the house from the pool. The women roll dangerously close to the garbage container. Augusta can smell the salty ocean, which she first thinks is seeping from the pool woman, until she remembers the shrimp she shelled for Tina's dinner last night.

The image of Tina sucking the butter off her fingers after eating shrimp brings no flashes of guilt to Augusta, even as Augusta licks the long thumb of the pool woman. Tina and Augusta are fervently nonmonogamous; guilt and jealousy have been exiled from their open marriage. Their only boundaries are the ethical ones born of their individual professions. Tina does not have sexual relations with her patients, at least not until the therapeutic relationship has been terminated for six months. Augusta does not have sexual relations with her students, at least not until the woman has graduated the college and there is no possibility the former student would be anything other than former.

Augusta's modus operandi is well established and well known. There is the casual meeting with promises to get together; the lunch date which ends with the invitation for dinner at the former student's house to show appreciation; the carefully cooked meal which leads to bed if the former student desires it, is previously lesbian, and does not have a live-in lover or a relationship with another student, former or otherwise. Then there is nothing else. Augusta likes to think of herself as a woman who does not flourish on the clutter of relationships. That is Tina's style.

The pool woman on the floor with Augusta for the first and what Augusta knows will be the last time is very very tan and slight. Augusta imagines that even the pool woman's bones are tan; that the long humerus which juts through the pool woman's elbow into Augusta's stomach is not bleached white as it would have been had it been exposed to the sun without the cover of muscle and flesh. Instead, the pool woman's bones are a hot, sweet shade of brown, like bones which had been buried in rich, wet soil and tunneled by hungry insects. Or so Augusta visualizes, as her own bones soften into flesh, as her own flesh solidifies into water.

It was before the two women made love that the pool woman had vacuumed. Augusta had watched the pool woman's thin muscled arms charm the long snakes of hose, wondering about the pool woman's childhood. She imagined that the pool woman came from a large family in Citrus or Orange counties; that the pool woman grew up expecting to marry a man like her father who worked as a supervisor in the orange and grapefruit groves. Or perhaps the pool woman had grown up on the coast, in a city like St. Augustine, learning to surf better than her brother and dreaming of finding a mermaid in the waves. Augusta knew she would never ask the woman anything, even if she had sex with her: what if the woman was from someplace like Cincinnati?

Augusta sat in a lounge chair, studying the pool woman, the pool, and the gray wall, wondering how wet the pool woman became during sex, and pretending to read a minor novel by a minor woman who would never rise to the fame of an entry on a women's studies syllabus. Augusta always intended to devote her summers to discovering undiscovered women and creating a course. But Augusta knew that as soon as she required her students to discover the woman, the woman was no longer undiscovered. Or, Augusta thought, she might be creating a totally new paradigm for teaching women's studies, something that transcended male-created disciplines like sociology and literature, transcended even male-defined categories like class and gender. But Augusta's summer never seemed long enough. It took months to bake and swim away the tension she collected during the academic year.

Tina indulged Augusta's lazy summers, perhaps even spawning them by her insistence on purchasing this house. "Why the hell live in Florida and not have a pool?" Tina had laughed. The house was inconveniently located, but no more so than almost every other house in the sprawling suburb of Orlando, which did not serve as a bedroom for a real city but as one for the fantasy world of tourist attractions. The house had no driveway, no trees in the front yard, and no character, but home ownership was vital to their view of themselves as a couple. It was also part of their view of themselves that Augusta was brilliant but brittle, and that Tina was a pragmatic caretaker. The caretaker was the one who convinced Augusta that she deserved to have a pool, although Tina herself could not swim. The caretaker was the one who prescribed nonmonogamy for Augusta's complexities, and Tina only engaged in it herself (or so she said) out of an excessive sense of fairness.

In the afternoon, after the pool woman is gone, Tina telephones the pool company to complain about the pool.

The pool has sediment on the bottom, sediment that the pool woman had promised would not reappear. It looks like a fine gray charcoal, like ashes sifted after a fire. The pool woman had explained to Augusta that the sediment was caused by a chemical reaction between the chlorine sticks and another compound she referred to by a splash of unrelated letters. Although Augusta could not remember the chemical's name, she remembered that it appeared on the service bill every month, remembered that it was white.

Augusta did not trust the pool woman's explanation because she did not trust chemistry: how could two virginally white substances combine to produce that sinister silt that shifted along the bottom of the pool?

Augusta had never studied chemistry in school. Once she had wanted a chemistry set for Christmas. She and her best friend, Kathy Daniels, each asked their mothers for one. What both of their mothers said was no, explaining that their daughters could blow up the entire apartment building. At first, both Augusta and Kathy thought that their mothers' fear was an excuse. Later, the girls overheard their mothers, best friends themselves, talking in one or the other of their narrow kitchens, sitting over cooling coffee, Duncan Hines chocolate cake, and cigarettes.

One mother had said, "Those girls could blow this whole entire building to Kingdom Come."

The other mother answered, "Jesus," almost laughing, but with a catch of fear deep in her smoke-filled throat.

The girls knew then that they would never be given chemistry sets. What the girls did get every June, on the last day of school, when they brought home their final report cards like passports to the country of the next grade, was a summer pass to Beginni's Swim Club, around the corner from the Newark, New Jersey apartment building. The mothers bought these passes for their daughters, even if the mothers could not afford luxuries for themselves, because the passes were not luxuries. The passes kept the daughters off the hot summer streets which might provoke rioting and out of the cool city stores which might prove tempting. The mothers were trying to protect their daughters from laws against breaching the peace and shoplifting; trying to protect their daughters from additional juvenile convictions. The mothers were also thinking that Beginni's Swim Club might keep their daughters safe from boys for another summer. The mothers had to work.

For several summers at Beginni's, the girls persisted in the magical safety purchased by their mothers. The girls held hands and kissed underwater. If anyone ever noticed, the observer thought of them not as potential sexual deviants but as playfully young domesticated animals, like kittens or puppies. The girls thought of themselves more as dolphins than kittens, and usually more as mermaids than as humans. They swam with their ankles crossed and their legs pressed tightly together. The chlorinated water rushing between their thighs and through their bathing suit bottoms gave them pleasure, but this pleasure was indistinct from other pleasures of the body, such as opening their eyes underwater or finally letting their lungs fill with air.

The mermaids were swimmers, but they also became adept at diving. They were coached by the lifeguards at Beginni's Swim Club and always entered into the Labor Day competitions which their mothers attended, cheering for their daughters. The lifeguards, who the girls thought of as *guys*, were doing daily laps between boyhood and manhood. These guys all had girlfriends upon whom they made sexual demands, although at least one of the guys was figuring out that he was more attracted to his fellow lifeguards than his girlfriend.

But the guys were more boys than men when they coached the mermaids. The only lust that ever made one of the guys touch the mermaids was the passion for the perfect dive. A lifeguard's hand on one of the girls' buttocks meant she needed to tuck before springing into the water, nothing more.

If any other male approached the girls, the mermaids pretended that they could not speak English, or any other language in which the male might be fluent. The mermaids conversed in a cross between the dolphin squeaks they heard on the television program "Flipper," and the Spanish, Yiddish, Russian, and Chinese they heard on the streets and within the walls of their own apartment building. Then they would swim underwater to a location upon which they had apparently agreed after much debate. If an unusual male was undeterred and pursued, he might find himself in the shadow of an overheated lifeguard who had decided to swim over to the girls with professionally menacing strokes. In the watery world of Beginni's Swim Club, the girls were as impervious to threats of rape as mermaids.

Their shimmering safety ended when the girls got older. It ended before the girls' bodies betrayed them with breasts that promised a voluptuousness worthy of any mermaid, before the newly hired lifeguards started to think of them as potential girlfriends, before the girls abandoned the language they had created. It ended when the law allowed them to apply for working papers.

Those summers in the unairconditioned clothing warehouse heaving autumn wools and corduroy made Kathy Daniels crazy enough to marry the first man who promised her that she would never have to work again. Those same summers, and the lonely one after Kathy got married, and the ones that seemed the same after Kathy got divorced, made Augusta think. Augusta thought about Kathy, moving nearby to the almost-suburb of West Orange (or was in South Orange?) which as Kathy reported had not a single orange tree, although there were wonderful yards; and about Kathy moving back to the almost-slum of her mother's apartment which as Kathy observed at least did not house some man trying to suck at her as if she was full of sweet juice. Augusta thought about their mothers working in the same warehouse, summers and winters and the seasons between.

Augusta thought about the women who would wear the heavy clothes she was picking for an order from a store in Oklahoma that would mark-up each item at least fifty percent; for an outlet in Idaho which sold second-quality merchandise and marked it up only forty-five percent. Augusta thought about women all the time. Certainly she thought about kissing them and being kissed by them, stroking them and being stroked by them, swimming with them in some body of water created solely for them. But Augusta also thought of women more abstractly. She thought of them in percentages of consumers who would choose the green wool-pleated skirt over the blue plain A-line. She thought of the women who would shoplift the lined winter coats. She thought of housewives reading novels and mistresses smoking cigarettes and girls who should be outside playing basketball but who fit themselves into kitchens to cook dinners. Sometimes she thought of women as chemicals capable of predictable reactions, if only she could discover the formula.

Augusta worked in the warehouse through high school, through college, through her Ph.D. in sociology at Rutgers. After the coursework and the dissertation ("Working Women in the Garment Trades, 1950-1965"), she quit the warehouse. After six years of teaching ("Women and Work," "The Literature of Working Women," "Women and the Economy"), she almost never thinks of the warehouse. She still thinks about women. She still thinks about sex with women. But she still mostly thinks about theoretical women—women who have no smell.

Stretched on a lounge by the pool, Augusta's mind is filled with patterns as abstract as the design on her bathing suit. She is watching the wind blow the furry mimosa leaves across the too-low wall and into the water when she sees the pool woman reappear through the gate. Augusta thinks that the pool woman is more narrow than she remembered, although it had only been this morning since the two women had tasted the faint spice of chlorine on each other's skin.

"You bitch," the pool woman hisses, walking on the deck toward Augusta.

"What's the matter?" Augusta asks, although she thinks she already knows. Augusta is a woman well trained in the danger of assumptions.

"The matter?" The pool woman sounds like an underwater echo, like Flipper reverberating in ultrasonic waves.

The pool woman comes closer. Augusta clumsily gets up from

the lounge. She looks at her watch, fastened around her sandal. She hopes that Tina will keep her promise to be home late. Augusta would be more embarrassed to be caught in a scene than in an embrace.

"I'll tell you what's wrong. I got fired. I got fired because some damn dyke I serviced on her kitchen floor after I serviced her pool called up and complained that I left sediment on the bottom. 'The bottom of what?' I ask the boss. 'The bottom of her high-and-mighty ass or the bottom of her pool?' 'What do you think?' he says. And then the prick fires me."

"I didn't mean for you to get fired."

"Oh, how nice. And I'm going to be just as nice. I'm here to clean the sediment from the bottom of your pool with your damn ass."

Augusta wonders whether or not she should resist the tan woman rushing toward her with the long-handled pool broom. Part of Augusta would love to glide underwater with the pool woman's tanness, almost like making love again. Part of Augusta doesn't want to get her hair wet this late in the afternoon.

Augusta does not remember deciding. All she remembers when she wakes up wet on the cement next to the lounger is that the pool woman was here, but now she is gone. Augusta slips on her sandals. The watch clicks on the ground as she walks. Augusta checks the side gate, cursing the pool woman for not closing it, but she does not close it herself.

Instead, Augusta walks to the bedroom she shares with Tina. She towels her hair but dresses without showering. She wears white cotton jeans, white sneakers, and a T-shirt she brought home for Tina from the ninth annual National Women's Studies Association conference. Augusta wants to go and get a new piece of clothing, something light and summery. Something nice. Something that will make Tina want to take her out to dinner, no matter how late Tina arrives home or where she has been.

Altamonte Mall, with its one hundred and six specialty shops and its five major department stores, floats in the middle of a whirlpool of traffic. Augusta is sucked safely to its center and finds an unshaded parking space identical to at least a thousand other slots painted onto the hot asphalt. Once this land had been devoted to groves, as Augusta knows from one of her published papers ("The Migrant Farmworker Woman in Florida: 1950-1965"). Augusta can picture the long rows of the popular Valencia and the profitable Hamlin orange trees, dotted with fruit that would be rapidly abandoning its greenness at this time of year. Soon, a grower in tepid gray Sansabelt slacks would walk among the trees, watching a migrant woman dive from her ladder for ripe fruits. Augusta imagined the noble lines of movement rippling from the woman's work; the grower was only a space covered with clothes. The grower further proved his ignominious greed by selling the land to developers, an even more vacuously despicable breed. Augusta mourned the loss of work for the migrant woman, a woman who probably would not fit the wholesome image required for even minimum-wage employment at any Magic Kingdom enterprise. Augusta does not think about the grower or the developer, except as conspirators to deprive all women of the sacred citrus groves. Augusta had never actually been in a grove, but she consoled herself that she had never been to Disney World either.

The mall is cool and crowded with people trying to escape the shimmering heat. Augusta remembers that her mother always said that five o'clock was the hottest part of the day. Augusta looks at the golden space on her arm where her watch should have been. The building is filled with girls mostly, Augusta notices; or perhaps Augusta notices only the girls. The mall as municipal swimming pool, Augusta thinks, as if it is the title of an article she read, or one she will think about writing.

It is a pale green-blue like reflected water. Light as a ripple across protected water. Soft as skin underwater. It is a blouse of washable silk. Affordable, really. On sale, even. The credit cards wait patiently in Augusta's wallet, next to the blank checks drawn on a joint account with a comfortable balance.

Augusta expertly shoplifts the blouse. The thrill of the threat of getting caught is mitigated by her professionalism. In another store, she buys, with cash, a scarf for Tina. Augusta never steals gifts.

She is glad when she sees Tina's Peugeot parked several houses down, with a parking space conveniently in front of it. As Augusta angles her car, she looks down at her new silk blouse. She hopes she is not sweating in it. Still, seeing Tina's car makes her glad that she changed into it at the mall bathroom.

But Tina is not home. Does not come to the door like she usually does. Or she is home, but is hiding. They do not know any neighbors. There is no place close enough to walk. She must be home. Augusta checks the bedroom. Her sandals are dry now, on the floor where she left them, the watch still attached by its strap. Tina is not napping on the bed. She is not in the bathroom where Augusta's swimsuit is draped on the towel rack. Augusta walks into the kitchen. She pushes past the garbage, slides open the glass door. Augusta enters the fast twilight.

From the edge of the concrete deck, Augusta sees a shadow. She squints at it. At first she thinks it is the sediment, collected into a shapeless monster at the deep end of the pool. She wonders if the shadow is too large to be one woman's body, too large to be only Tina, too large to be only the pool woman.

Augusta looks at the wall. She thinks about women: about women's clothes, about women's work, about women's childhoods. She thinks about women's bodies; about sinking, about breathing water, about waiting to be buoyed by death. Then she dives into the pool, her ankles crossing like the memory of a mermaid, her silk blouse clinging to the memory of air.

# LISTEN TO THE DANCE OF THE MANGO

## ENSEMBLE

We are not natives.

We were grafted and transplanted for generations. Like slaves or the unwed daughters of immigrants, we were not asked if we would like to resettle. But now that we are here, we live our long lives as if we have chosen the soil which our roots suck.

As if we had chosen to leave the true tropics, where the warmth of the day and the cool of the night are vaster in change than the seasons of summer and winter. We birthed our fruit when we chose. It could be five months or five years. We could bear five fruit or five thousand.

We could dance. Pregnant and heavy with orange ovoid bulbs, or covered only with leaves lighter than the humid air, we danced. And the people came to us reverently and danced with us. They seduced our fruit and dripped its stringy juice on our roots as they ate mango after mango. They clapped and chanted and danced until the world was a fever. They honored our long thick pits by burying them in a pile of their own excrement.

We grew and our children grew. We grew until our leaves spread green as eternity, until we looked like continents bold as Africa against an ocean-blue sky. We grew and we danced in our native lands.

Here, north of the tropic zone, we continue to dance. In impromptu groves, in neighborhood yards, across the street from schools, we dance. It is sometimes thought that we have been cultivated here, that we are no longer wild, but this is thought only by those who have never heard us dance. Those pale people who stay in their houses never hear the rhythms of our growth, a grand pas de deux of control and abandon. Our costumes rustle with new leaf apple red and a hint of virgin purple; with mature leaf vibrant green and healthy bark cocoa brown; with ravishing ripe fruit mango orange. Some shut their windows against the calls of our mating, as our limbs caress themselves with graceful and passionate embraces. We are each of us complete, each of us perfect.

But we are not natives. As if to remind us, the winter unleashes its biting powers against us. We hear people say it is the coldest weather in a century, but many of us are older than that and we cannot remember it ever being this cold. We hear that men are being paid to protect the citrus from the winter, to keep the profits from being frozen. But we are not commercial enough to inspire such care. We are freezing.

Our leaves are chewed by the frost and burned a shriveled brown. The bitter wind tears through us like a crazed rapist shredding paperthin underpants. We shiver with the inevitability of victims.

It is useless to dance; our movements would only whip the cold air faster. The sun seems to mock us, for it is not strong enough to thaw us. The night becomes a brutal enemy.

We are holding our ground. But there are those among us who say we are doomed.

## INTERLUDE

I am a native. I was born in a nursery a bit north of here, hatched from a split seed and grafted to perfection.

She bought me from a discount store when I was an infant. She brought me here, where we lived together for seventeen years. We have watched each other grow. I have peeked through the windows she always leaves open and I have seen her cook and clean and sleep. Then she gets in a little brown car and drives away, returning only at dawn.

In the mornings, her white cheeks would be streaked with black and her mane would tangle past her shoulders. She would come to me then and lean her body against mine. The mockingbirds would sit in my branches and sing for both of us. She knew how to be silent, how to listen.

She is not like some of our neighbors who come to the subtropics from a colder zone and attempt to make this land like the land they escaped. She came from somewhere else. She sometimes read letters from people far away while she sat in the shade of my leaves, but she has made this our home. She lives like I do.

Everyone loves someone who lives like herself, and I loved her. I still do, which makes her betrayal bitter, bitter and cold as the harshest winter in a century.

I froze but I survived. She trimmed the dead burned leaves from me, and I gathered my strength. I can feel the ripples of my pregnancy and know I will give birth to fruit this summer, as I do every summer, a rarity for a tree of my breed. I bear because I love to feel her hand close around the speckled bulb of fruit and pull it to her mouth. I love to watch her teeth nick the skin and then her lips suck the almost-sweet juice. I bear because I love her.

It is because I love her that I cannot bear what is happening to me, what she is allowing to happen. The men in the dark-green uniforms are here. They have come to chop me down because I interfere with their lines. They have come to uproot me, to destroy me, to murder me.

She does not run outside to protect me. I have always been there when she needed me, and now she is betraying me. I have always watched over her. I have seen so much of her life.

Perhaps that is it—I have seen too much of her life. Perhaps I no longer remind her of our beauty, but only of the ugliness of a half-moon ago.

There were men in green uniforms then. Four of them. Three were almost as pale as she, and one was much darker. They all had big hands and big teeth and loud voices. The tallest one held her down by the window, and the other three tore off her clothes. Then one by one they bounced and heaved their bodies on top of the full length of her. I could hear her screams, though she made no sounds. Then the tallest one pulled her outside and pushed her face into the cement of the back stoop and threw his body onto her.

When they were gone she crawled over to me, and I could see she was bleeding. I wished I had branches that could bend down and cradle her. Instead, I could only listen to her sob.

At first I thought it was the same men who had returned to attack me, but the uniforms are a different shade of green. They measure me with their eyes just like the other men measured her, though. I can see why she doesn't protect me. She must be afraid.

When I see that she is crying, I know I am doomed.

# SOLO

She is not a native. She came here thirty years ago, married to a gambling good-looking man long-since dead. He was shot through the chest in the Tropical Breezes Club while she was on the stage dancing and shaking for tips. The music was pounding in her ears so loud she hardly heard the gun. There was very little commotion. The bartender and bouncer were efficient. Everything was cleaned up and she was let go, under the circumstances.

Grief was the only thing that kept her from getting a job the next day, for her trade was one which was in demand in the many new clubs opening up on what was being called the gold coast. When mourning was replaced by the incessant knocking of the landlord, she went to another club and was immediately hired. She used her husband's scant insurance money for a down payment on a little stucco house. For years she traveled the circuit, dancing at one club and then the next, leaving for better pay, greater protection, the promise of bigger tips or a notion of a better class of club.

But it was not so easy now. What they see when she applies for a job is only that she is not young. Though she can look any man in the eye and say she is thirty-nine, even her lie does not put her in the category of the most desirable. She wears a long fall of blondish curls, top and bottom eyelashes, and synthetic nails.

In the darkness, with a red light and then a green light flashing across her milky body, she is nearly beautiful. There is no doubt she can dance. Men who have no notion of grace have been heard to remark on her talent. Her ballet legs, earned in years of training that her immigrant mother paid for by sewing lacy blouses in factories, still serve her well. The perfection in the tautness of her muscles and in the strict shape of her bones cannot be tarnished by patches of cellulite or a too-blue bulge of vein.

So she still makes good tips and won't work in a place where the management allows the customers to "paw the girls." She has standards and a sense of morals upon which she prides herself. She will say that she has been around too long not to value the truth.

Which is why, when she was asked about the tumble in the Paradise Lounge parking lot, she told how the sheriffs took turns beating the Black kid and then shot him in the back as he ran. She gave a sworn statement to the state attorney. She allowed herself to be interviewed on TV. She knew it was only a matter of time before they came for her.

Yet she was more worried about the damn mango tree in her backyard. She'd been fighting with the power company for three years about that tree. She was careful to always keep it trimmed, to keep its lushness from tangling with the power lines that she knew were too low. She thought that the freeze would stunt the tree, but it only seemed to grow more. She'd argued and protested, but now the power company had gotten orders from the county. They were going to chop the tree down. She couldn't see a way not to submit. She'd even been to a lawyer.

It seemed suddenly as if all the power in the world was against her, and she felt doomed.

## ENCORE

The mango trees froze. Gradually the warm air came, tentative as a guilty lover who knows the absence cannot be excused. The trees opened themselves and allowed their bodies to brim with the most gentle of greens. They whirled away those crinkled dervishes that were once mature leaves. They did not mourn as the moistureless appendages fell from them and rolled like cured cattle tongues across neatly fenced prairie lawns. They sloughed off the waves of the dead and turned their tides inward, higher and higher, until they swelled with life.

A mango tree was chopped down. The power company's buzz saw roared through the bark as if it were paper. The roots were not bothered. The tree could not believe its fortune, but it kept quiet until it was sure the air was warm and spring could not be killed. It was then that the tree burst forth with tiny curled purple leaf, then a reddish one. It was then that it revealed herself before the woman and heard the woman cry out in joy. The woman danced, and the tree danced with her. They whirled until the neighborhood was filled with the power of their music.

She was raped. She lost her job because no one wants a bruised dancer, or a dancer with a noticeably missing tooth. She testified in a courtroom full of men who leered at her. When they asked her what her occupation was, she said that she no longer danced. But even then, she knew that was not true. For she danced at night in her little stucco house with the windows pushed open by the smell of jasmine. She danced and danced when she saw that her mango tree was alive and singing with pirouettes of little leaves. She danced when the jury found the sheriffs not guilty and when the state attorney said there was no protection for her. She danced when she applied for a waitress job. She dances still, and the mango trees dance with her. Survival is their dance, and their dance is survival. Listen to the subtropics hum with it.

# LIVES OF A LONG-HAIRED LESBIAN: FOUR ELEMENTAL NARRATIONS

## HOME FIRES

It wasn't the fire that killed her, although it could have been. It could have killed me, too. It could have killed the woman upstairs with the baby daughter whose hair was just getting long enough to curl. But the fire didn't kill anyone, unless you count the sluggish roaches, which I don't.

There are years before the fire. These years, like all the years of my lifetime, have numbers: 1971 or 1973 or 1974 or 1970. It is after 1967, because Wade is always saying, "Girls, it ain't 1967 anymore." He says this because of how we look. We like to think Wade is a good friend. Wade isn't our friend, he is our pimp.

Wade is always interested in the way we dress, which makes him seem like a friend. I almost always wear a black fitted-bodice leotard, Danskin style 268. I wear it with size 28 Levi jeans or a black-and-mauve Indian print cotton shirt, depending on the weather. Stacie always wears a green turtleneck, regardless of the weather. She usually pulls on size 27 jeans, although she also has a jean skirt and a pair of tight-fitting overalls. We wear flat sandals. Wade always nags us about our shoes. He advises, "High heels are hot." We pretend we are naive.

Stacie keeps her hair long and blonde because men like it that way. That's what she says. Wade approves. I don't understand why men like it that way; I've never understood anything about men. My hair is actually longer, but Stacie is shorter, so her hair looks longer. Or maybe my hair looks shorter because it is the color of ashes rather than the color of straw. We are white. We have blue eyes that border on green. We are young. I am always younger.

In summer, we practice being thin. We live on black beauties, water, and bananas. Someone had told Stacie that it was impossible to starve to death if one ingested enough potassium. Bananas are the best source of potassium. Stacie calls bananas the yellow flames of life. We eat them incessantly. We always eat them sliced.

In winter, we walk the streets past the men who burn fires in trash cans to keep warm. They call out to us. Sometimes we wave. Sometimes we call back. We always keep moving, fast in our flat sandals. We must be cold.

There are several summers and seemingly many more winters. We move around. Wade follows us or finds us places to live. The rooms are the narrowest of hallways or bleed into one another without definition. We have wicker furniture and posters and three ceramic bowls and a hurricane oil lamp given to us by Stacie's sister and some knives. We have candles and incense and a lighter from Pakistan. We have flower pots filled with soil and seed which we move from windowsill to windowsill. We have one bed, one set of safari animals sheets, two pillows, and a quilt made in Georgia. We have each other.

We are more than lovers. We are mirrors. We are closer than twins. We are two halves craving wholeness. We are lost princesses. We aren't sure what to call ourselves. We say *roommates*. We say *partners*. Wade says, *Whatever turns you on, girls.*

We want a different life. We sit in the kitchen of Stacie's married sister, Brenda. Brenda says, *Get a straight job.* I moan that I can't type. Stacie complains because she doesn't have the right clothes. We decide to become waitresses.

The cocktail lounge is dark. It is hard not to whore. The bartender keeps setting me up with tricks. Men scrape twenty-dollar bills across my fishnet stockings. Stacie works a split shift. The bartender comes home with me, but he is impotent. He gives me a ten-dollar bill, and I give it back. Wade comes to the lounge and threatens to break both of Stacie's wrists. We quit.

We start doing Tarot cards, as if to convince ourselves we have a future. Our favorite suit is wands. It seems the most magical and yet the most familiar. We dabble in astrology. Stacie is an Aries with a Leo moon and Sagittarius rising. I had lied about my birthdate for so long, I cannot remember any of the vital information. We begin to talk about moving somewhere very far away. Like Florida. Or New Mexico. Or an island.

A lavender candle tips onto a wicker table. The landlord's insurance agents will try to decipher the shards of a hurricane oil lamp. We will tell them that it never had any oil, but they will not believe us. They will not believe how I pulled Stacie through a flaming window frame. They will not believe that I thought she must be dead. They will not believe how her hair singed to the roots in places, because by the time they see her, I have chopped it short and defiant.

Wade finds us another place to live. I can't sleep without the safari sheets. Stacie won't eat any bananas. We always think we smell smoke. We try to quit cigarettes. She cries into my shoulder. "Anna, I need to escape from all this shit." I don't describe how the promise of asphyxiation had lulled me. I don't tell her that only when I thought of her also dying had I been able to wake myself up.

Stacie disappears on her seventeenth birthday. It is spring. I finally find her at her sister's house. I knew Brenda and her husband were away for three weeks, so I hadn't looked there earlier. Stacie is hanging from the dining room light fixture. I can see her through the window. I long for the Pakistani lighter. I decide the only thing I could do was set Brenda's house on fire. But I don't.

Instead I change my name to Anastasia, after the mysterious survivor of the execution of the Czar's entire family, after Stacie, after myself.

Instead I hitchhike to Florida. Or New Mexico.

Instead I go to the store and buy a pack of cigarettes and a can of lighter fluid. I take three extra boxes of matches.

Instead I head for Wade's duplex.

## LAVENDER OCEANS

Sometimes a bed seems like an island. It's best if it's raining through an open window, and the surrounding carpet is blue, and if you're sharing a clean quilt with someone who shares your sexual proclivities.

My island had seemed like a desert since Effie had gone back to Athens. I had met her at a rally and fallen in love with her dark and downy moustache. Her two-week tour turned into a nine-month residence at my stark apartment. Three seasons can be a long time. They can also be awfully short.

I missed her so much I couldn't look at another woman.

It is raining, and the windows are open. Drops of water stray past my eyebrows, but they could be sweat. The rug is not blue, it is lavender. Still, any color ocean will do, especially since I'd landlocked myself into New Mexico.

The quilt is clean. We share it quite nicely, for we are used to sharing. We'd spent years sharing: platforms, funds, derision, dinners, clothes. As coordinators of the Organization for Unity Among Lesbians and Gay Men, we'd fought many battles together. We'd even fought each other. We were confident we could survive together on a desert island.

But we would have sooner thought we'd be stranded in the Agean than in bed together. We share the same sexual proclivity, in a sense: the sense which guides us away from each other. Our proclivity is toward similarity rather than not. Our passion is reserved for our own genders. Side by side, we seem embarrassingly disparate.

I hadn't been in bed with a man since I was fifteen-and-a-half-years old. Before then, I'd been with enough men to last me several long lifetimes. But I don't think I'd ever been in bed wearing only one pink sock with a man wrapped in a scarf (mine?). As far as I know, Christopher doesn't make a habit of this sort of thing either.

Here we are. The rain. The lavender ocean. The clean quilt. Our earrings clink against each other. A crisp tongue runs along my fisted knuckles. I scratch an edge of beard and ear. The hairs on our shins ruffle.

"Relax," he says. He begins to massage my back, my neck, my face, and then my head. "Relax your skull," he says. "Is it relaxed? I can't feel it under all that hair. It's weird being so close to someone with all that hair on their head."
"All my lovers say that."
"You know, the first time I saw you, at the Pride March meeting, years ago, I couldn't figure you out because of that hair."
"All my lovers say that."
"Are we lovers?" he asks.
"I don't know."
We float. We sink. I cannot understand what is happening.

If Chris is a man, then I must be a man.

If I am a woman, then Chris must be a woman.

An anthropologist might call this sex. A sociologist might not.

We get up and swim to the shower together. We know better than to argue with either anthropologists or sociologists. Besides, we have a lot of work to do. We must organize a benefit for a Lesbian mother fighting a custody battle.

"Anastasia, Anastasia," he calls from across the room, as if we had not seen each other for seasons instead of having parted that very morning. We abandon a meeting to look for a bottle of wine. We hold hands on the street, both casually and furtively. We go back to the meeting with the wine. I make an inexcusably early exit and walk home. I call Effie in Athens. She is busy and will return my transatlantic call some other time.

I am wearing my hair tucked into a madras hat and watching a softball game when I meet Cora Mae. She is playing first base. She has an infant packed on her back and a cropped Afro. I think she is beautiful. I try to figure if the baby means she isn't a Lesbian.

She is. A wonderful one. But she is just passing through New Mexico on her way to stay with her sister in California, although she decides to pass through a little longer. Her baby, Jasmine, sleeps on the island of a bed with us, while Cora Mae and I lick each other nearly senseless. We give each other and Jasmine sweet-smelling baths. We powder each other with English lavender which splatters on the rug. She pushes two fingers so deeply into me that my back arches into a circle and I fill the bed with wetness. We talk about our dead parents, about being survivors, about being natural Lesbians unwilling to adopt every convention of the life we had chosen. She has her baby. I have my hair.

When she leaves it is raining. I telephone Effie in Athens but disconnect the line before anyone answers. That night it is still raining. I run into Chris at a meeting. He has shaved his head, his beard. We go out for a bottle of wine. We find a sharp white bordeaux. I buy a bunch of almost-ripe bananas. He buys a bunch of grocery store flowers. We walk back to my place. The windows are open. The rug is still lavender.

He starts to massage my neck, but I ask him to come inside me instead. In am incredulous at my own invitation. He debates, then pulls me on top of him. "Only if it's like this," he says. I nod. My hair falls around his desert-flat chest.

In the morning, he tells me his dreams. He dreamed of a forest, of a woman with long hair who could have been me but wasn't, of someone dancing.

I tell him I dreamed of a pale purple sea. But I had dreamed of his sister. But I had dreamed of Cora Mae and Effie and Stacie. I had dreamed of lighting a fire in the crawlspace of a duplex. I dreamed I had been a Lesbian so long I forgot about birth control.

# GAEA

Karma lost her shoe. Her mother is standing at the door waiting for me to find it. She comes during lunch to take her child to a doctor's appointment and assumes her child needs both shoes. There are forty cardboard lockers to inspect. Neither Karma nor her mother are helping. The children eat their rice innocently.

I'd been working at Ocala Day School for quite a while, living in a trailer in the woods. There are more woods in Florida than most people think. I take the children on walks and pretend we are a tribe lost in some wonderful wilderness.

While I rub the backs of the children to induce the *nap* in the scheduled naptime, I daydream of a Greek island. I imagine myself walking through an olive grove on Lesbos. I'd read that the island is called Mytilene now, I guess for the obvious reasons. It is for those same obvious reasons that I want to suck the pits out of olives in those groves.

While I rub the back of Shatki, an un-nappably vibrant four-year-old, I daydream of her mother. Ora has the reddest and shortest hair of any woman I'd ever seen. I can almost see the freckles on her skull. She has freckles everywhere else, or so I imagine. I wonder if she is a Lesbian.

No one else in these woods seems to be. It is hard to live here. I have a crush on Diana, the director of the day school, but she is heartlessly heterosexual. Her husband, Davie, is the school's accountant. He brings her lunch every day. Diana's sister, the assistant director, tells me she thinks Davie is sweet. I think he is sickening. I try not to watch him as he presses his hand between Diana's legs, pulling them apart. I try not to watch him kiss her neck, crumbs of his lunch still on his moustache.

I sit outside and draw my names in the lush dirt with a stick, while the children sleep, each on her or his own mat. The trees beyond the school's clearing look like a green net, like a verdant web. I am sitting on the outermost string, if I am connected at all. It is easy to pity myself because every other woman in the world seems to have a sister.

At 6:00 p.m., closing time on the day that Karma's mother said she would not drop the matter of the unmated shoe, I stand by the gate with ten children. They are all mud-caked and weary. One of them unscrambles himself from the group to pull at my beige camp shorts. For the first time in eight hours, I recognize this creature with blond curls as my son. That leaves nine children waiting for parents.

At twenty minutes past six, the director and assistant director long-since departed, only Shatki is left by the gate with Colin and me. I decide to take a risk. I put a note on the door and take Shatki to my trailer. Colin is thrilled. He always loves company, any company, but he is especially impressed with the older girl of auburn hair and green eyes.

I stand in the middle of my bedroom, debating whether or not to put Shatki into the bed where Colin and I usually sleep. We have already eaten, already done Colin's two puzzles several times each, already had baths and snacks. I stand there for a long time, with two confused preschoolers, until Ora knocks on the dark door. She'd had truck trouble on a distant road. She is hauling landfill these days. She is appropriately apologetic and grateful. She invites Colin and me for dinner.

I am surprised to find she is a good cook. It is "just one of my hobbies," she says. For desert she makes bananas flambé. I wince at the flames. She holds my plate close to my face, thinking she is teasing me. The children laugh.

Later, when the children are snoring in Shatki's bunk beds, we sweat between Ora's jungle-patterned sheets. I blanch when she wants to tie my hands with scarves. Her loving is opulent and virulent. I am shy.

"I suppose with a name like Anastasia, you're afraid of a lot of things," she says softly.

"My real name is Anna," I tell her for no reason.

She continues to call me Anastasia.

Her house is cedar. I love the windows with stained glass flowers. She calls me her lover, her sister. I love that too. She has to be on the road, hauling, some nights until late. It seems sensible that I watch Shatki and Colin at a cedar house rather than a rusted trailer. It seems strange to continue to work at the Ocala Day School for minimum wage. I quit.

She likes to drink Rolling Rock beer and she likes to talk. She tells me my hair is too burdensome and she threatens to hack it off. She tells me I am too fat and my muscles are flaccid. She says I am too tame in bed. She tells me I am an earth mother and the children love me. She tells me she will kill me if Shatki ever calls me Mommy. She tells me she is the toughest bulldagger I will ever know, and if she catches me cheating, she will break my wrists. She tells me when Colin is sixteen, he will be a man and will have to move out. She tells me I treat him like a minor god, and he will eat me alive.

We are walking in the woods. We are arguing. She walks fast in her expensive sneakers. I skip in my flat sandals to keep her pace.

She pushes me harder than she means to. I fall on my face in the path. A branch bends into my neck. I do not try to get up. The earth smells like music. I can feel the vibrations of dancing under the ground.

I spend the seasons growing. I plant bulbs and flowers. I keep an impressive compost pile. I foster enormous cabbages. I tend tomatoes and sweet onions. I have vibrant azaleas. I learn to love color. I wear fuchsia blouses and purple pants. I buy the children rainbows of clothes in a thrift shop. I steal a batiked cap and stuff my hair into it.

After we harvest the last of the squash, she tells me I have to move. Her husband is returning from Canada.

# AEROBICS

All the walls are windowless and mirrored. Even the door is mirrored. I stand in front of the room, in my black fitted-bodice leotard and white sweat pants, rolling my neck and then my shoulders. I kick my legs; I squat; I press my elbows together. I breathe through my nose and exhale through my mouth. I shout encouragement. I push the stray hairs from my forehead.

My son brings me lunch on his pink bike. There is cheese and retsina and hard bread. We sit on the rocks outside the studio and talk. He speaks the language like a native. He is teaching himself to read with myths. He asks me hundreds of questions. "Who's Medusa, Momma?" he says. "Who's Antigone?" "What's a phoenix?" Sometimes I know the answers.

In midsummer, we sleep in our open-windowed house almost on the water and wait for the Meltemi winds to wake us. The light from the sea is lavender at dawn. We are warm. We wear open-weave clothes and strapped sandals. I twist my hair and pin it to my head like a pastry.

In winter, there are fewer tourists and the boats run less frequently. The air is sharper and only slightly colder. I sleep later and have dreams of beautiful deserts. My son tells me he dreams of lush forests and eating bananas. If it is especially damp, we share a blanket. I let a braid dangle down my back.

When I first arrived in this tideless part of the world, I turned my passion outward. I feigned love with every woman I touched. I caressed their skins like flames. I even attempted love with two men. The second one tore a fistful of my hair and then tried to pay me for the damage he had done. He never sent me flowers.

But now that I have been here season after season, I do not suffer such distractions. I am as calm as the winds. Calmer. I know the women of this island. The women of the island know me.

Most of the women who come to my classes want thinner thighs or flatter stomachs or bodies like young boys. They are tourists or wives of local merchants or waitresses or artists. Some of the women come to these classes for the reasons I teach them: I want women to be strong.

I make the women use weights. I work their biceps, their triceps, their wrists. I make them punch the air. I make them swing and twist and kick and jump. I tell them to pretend the air is water and they are swimming. I teach them resistance. I let them sweat.

I tell my students to call me Anemone. They tell me this means *windflower.* I call my studio Aerobics. This means *air,* I tell them. Soon, I tell them, we will be as light as air, as fresh as air, as free as air.

I watch my limbs tighten and strengthen. I watch my muscles harden. I watch the women in the room watch themselves in the mirrors. I watch some women more than others.

At first I think the two women are lovers. They have honey hair waved short to their scalps. I learn their names are Crystal and Melissa. Crystal is a sculptor and Melissa is a painter. They say they are English, and that since I have an awfully American accent, we must be cousins. They wear sleeveless leotards in identical Capezio pink. I almost envy them. They tell me they are sisters.

Crystal is a Lesbian. The way she stands, the direct gaze of her eyes, her laugh, tell me this. If I were still taking lovers, I would take Crystal. Instead, I work with her on her neck muscles. I massage. I prescribe exercises. She tells me her neck is weak from an adolescent accident.

Melissa is getting married to a Canadian photographer. She wants her stomach flat and unnaturally tight to camouflage any memories of pregnancies. She is letting her hair grow. She is thinking of moving to Athens.

An agent from Athens calls me about selling the business. I have to think a few seconds before I can decipher her English. I am distracted by her voice. I can recognize a former lover, even long distance. I know she will not remember me, I lived in New Mexico then. I am thankful for her fluency because she uses words like *lucrative* and *good will*. I say I have always been one to consider any offer. Her offer is worth considering.

I announce to the students that I am selling the school. I rent another house. I move outside of the village, higher on a hill, closer to the sky. My son and I discuss whether the air is truly clearer up here, or whether it only seems that way.

Melissa sits inside my new whitewashed walls and cries. I look out the window at the pale flowers blooming close to the ground. Sometimes Melissa drifts into sleep, but wakes herself again with sobbing. After two nights, she is able to tell me what is wrong. Her sister and her husband are lovers. She spends a few days deciding which one she hates more, whose betrayal is more heinous. When she says she would like to bury them alive, to set them on fire, to dump them into the sea, I do not believe her.

Instead, I believe we do not know what to do with our love for each other.

Instead, I believe we must learn that we do not have to *do* anything with our love for another.

Instead, I believe we must learn to love, and we must learn to do things; to accept connections but not to expect them.

I am thinking of learning herbs. I am thinking of polishing stones. I am thinking of becoming a long-haired Crone. I decide to make feather earrings to sell to tourists. I would like to learn the flute.

The agent comes to my house with final papers. She looks at me and looks at me. Then she looks at my son, shakes her head, but then looks at me again. I inspect her downy moustache. I take off my cotton hat and the ends of my hair follow gravity to my knees. She gasps and coughs to hide her surprise. In her cosmopolitan Greek, she says I seem familiar to her. She says she must have met my sister somewhere in her travels. In my horrid pronunciation and terrible grammar, I say that is impossible. I say I am my only sister.

# HER
# AND
# GERONIMO

October marks the beginning of the season in Indian River County, Florida: the rainy season, the citrus season, the tourist season. During the season, the lands between the Indian River and the Atlantic Ocean are flooded with migrant farmworkers from the South and retirees escaping the cold of the North.

Claire comes with the retirees, although strictly speaking she is not one of them herself. She comes with her husband, Mortimer, a semiretired dentist in Chicago who believes himself transformed into a fisherman when he is in Florida.

Geronimo comes with the migrants, although strictly speaking he is not one of them himself. He is a crewleader, a labor contractor, just as his father had been. Unlike his father, Geronimo tries to be fair and keep the migrants' pay from falling too far below the minimum wage.

Both Geronimo and Claire come to Indian River each October, at least in some measure, to see Sylvana. Claire vacations at Sylvana's Trade Post Campground, with its authentic-looking cabins and man-made well-stocked pond where Mortimer fishes. Geronimo sells the excess oranges and grapefruits his workers have picked to Sylvana's

Trade Post Fruit Company, a tourist trap perched alongside U.S. Highway 1. Both Claire and Geronimo share Sylvana's bed in the erratic
intervals she dictates.

It is the promise of Sylvana's vagrant passion that excites Geronimo
and Claire as they pull off the road into the imported gravel of Sylvana's parking lot for the first time this season. Separated in time
by a few hours, and in style by the virtues of a yellow Mercedes con-
trasted with the romance of a red Ford pickup, Claire and Geronimo
are both greeted by the same scene. The Trade Post Fruit Company
is occupied by a few desultory teenagers arranging oranges. About
one hundred and fifty yards to the southeast, the cabins look clean,
but virtually deserted. In the middle, the house boasts a spot of bright
color sitting in Sylvana's spot under the orange awning. Both Geronimo
and Claire are disappointed that it is not Sylvana but Bilma leaning
back on the steps in a persimmon caftan.

Bilma sports the honeyed tan and accent of a boat-lift Cuban.
She has never been a rich woman and therefore loves gold, which
she wears in dozens of chains around her neck and wrists. She does
maintenance and more and more management for Sylvana, who teases
her about the jewelry but never forgets to commemorate an occasion
with fourteen-carat links. Bilma is not an unfriendly person, but she
shuns both Claire and Geronimo, evading their questions about
Sylvana's whereabouts.

"¿Dónde está ella?"

Geronimo acts as if Bilma cannot speak perfect English. Or perhaps he thinks his use of Spanish will forge a connection on which
Bilma will slide him the answer. If he only knew. Bilma finds his Spanish
torturous. His native language is Mayan, which he speaks to some
of his laborers. It is a language of agriculture. And poverty. It is full
of pretty sounds and has seven seasons. But Geronimo thinks Spanish is the language of culture, and seduction. English is for important business.

"Her-on-ee-mo!"

Bilma pronounces Geronimo's name correctly, starting with its
Spanish *h* sound and including the *i* like a very long *e*. Still, she says
it like a reproach, as if to ask *donde* were an intimate question about
one's mother. His huge shoulders lump toward his chest and he looks

like a cowering bird. Once, Bilma had referred to him as a good-looking vulture who had obviously done a lot of body-building, and Sylvana had laughed.

When Claire comes to Bilma, she avails no strategies. She can speak only English and does not see the need to know any other language. She also does not see the need to cajole a mere maid. In her world, she is the one who is catered to—by Mortimer and by their son, Roger. Though she will admit Indian River seems to be a different world than Chicago. Even Mo is a bit more distant here, preoccupied with his hooks and baits. She has, on occasion, found herself cajoling Sylvana. But a maid? No, she will not sink that low.

Finally, in the second scorching week of October, Sylvana replaces Bilma on the steps of the house. Sylvana had used the weeks since she had come back from Blue Cypress Lake like a washrag, scouring the exhilarating stain of summer off her body. But she is getting older and does not work as fast as she did thirty years ago when she first started visiting the old woman, who was old even then. Also, Sylvana's flesh is less obliging now, and its crevices need to be coaxed to yield to autumn.

While Sylvana scrubbed and thought of the old woman, Geronimo and Claire have been circling the house, evading each other, exchanging polite words, their reconnaissance never ceasing. For more years than either would like to remember, they have been surveying each other's terrain at the trade post, each knowing that the other had a special relationship with Sylvana and each suspecting the intimacy. Both of them damned their own insecurity which would not allow them to risk upsetting the fragile balance with any demand for honesty or fidelity. This autumn, they track each other like two starving cats trying to be casual. The competition is fierce to see who will get to Sylvana first.

It is Geronimo.

He comes upon Sylvana brushing her hair outside as she always does, cleaning the boar-bristle brush with her fingers and giving the fine tangle of darkness to the wind.

"For the birds, for nests," she says, though he hardly hears her. Her long strands cling to the wooden steps like a loose bouquet of industrially thin wires. She never braids her hair; it is her vanity.

"Do you want to go to Sebastian?"

He has gained his composure and is determined to act as if they have been separated for a few moments rather than a few seasons.

"What for?"

She doesn't like to travel unless she has a reason, and loving Geronimo is not reason enough.

"To drink. To dance. To catch up on the news and spend my new money."

She goes inside to change her shirt and brush off her pants, clean this morning. He does not follow her, but keeps his left boot on the step, wary of Claire.

Only when they are on the highway several miles north of the trade post does Geronimo settle into his success and relax his guard. He feels like he is dreaming. A usually attentive driver, Sylvana has to remind him to flick his windshield wipers on.

The bar is not crowded; the downpour is not good for business. They both drink too fast and are too shy to dance in the lonely wooden space set aside on the floor for just that purpose. Besides, there is no music. They go to another bar, not because they want more noise, but because they want to feel less obvious. It is equally uncrowded. They drink too fast again, and again they do not dance. But they touch more and more.

Back in the truck, Geronimo asks Sylvana what she did at the lake this summer.

"Nothing much."

"For four months you did nothing much?"

He thinks he is teasing her, but she is neither enticed nor provoked.

"What's to do at Blue Cypress Lake?"

Her eyes glitter like those of the old woman, and she sees that Geronimo can be callous as well as stupid. But she thinks that she might still love him. So many years must mean something. The sharp rationales for their loving have been sanded down like the rain and wind must have sanded down the land that has become the flatness between the river and the ocean.

"You're right. Nothing much."

But he knows she was doing something. The same thing she does every summer, though he has no idea what that could be. Why go to a lake when the ocean is practically in your backyard? He is annoyed and fascinated with Sylvana's predictable eccentricities. They are something he admires in the same way he admires the way her jeans fit or the way she swings her hair. He cannot imagine Sylvana apart from him. Because he does not want to.

The lights are off in the house as well as in all of the cabins, including the one shared by Claire and Mo. Geronimo notices that Sylvana has abandoned her shoes as she pads across the long yard filled with mud. This time, he follows her up the stairs.

She lights a candle and lies across her double bed diagonally. He sits on the edge of the bed, each of his huge hands holding one of her feet. Stroking. Stroking. The smell of scotch blends with the ozone. Rain splatters through a window which Sylvana never closes. The rhythm of the water is its own intoxication.

Wet and sweet, they kiss like old friends.

Until the friendship gets wetter and sweeter and makes Geronimo's fingers clutch Sylvana's hair at the nape of her neck. Tightly. Almost too tightly. He is hissing at her.

*"Puta, puta. Lo que tu necessita es un buen rabo.* A good cock. My cock. And you need a fast fuck, too, don't you, *maricona?"*

She is twisting as if to be free but making no move to untangle herself. She is sweating and he is sweating. He is calling her *cono.* Cunt, cunt. He is taking off her jeans and telling her she is a *resingada.* One who has been fucked a lot. He is mixing up his Spanish and his English and forgetting Mayan. He is forgetting where he has been since the last time he left this bed.

Sylvana arches her back and says, *"quiero templarte."* I want to fuck you."

And they do. They do.

It is still raining before dawn when Geronimo leaves for the labor camp. He is proud that he is a man with responsibilities, and to wake up with a woman ten years older than himself on a Wednesday morning is not one of them. Even as he says this to himself, he does not believe it. All day, the branches of the citrus trees remind him of the tangle of Sylvana's hair against the sky blue of her sheets.

Sylvana is drinking tea at her laminated table when Claire's knock interrupts Bilma's shout that Claire is here.

"C'mon in."

Sylvana means both of them, but Bilma leaves to check on some reported roof leaks. The touristas in the cabins must be kept content.

"Where have you been?"

Claire can sense that Geronimo has beaten her once again to Sylvana's bed, and she cannot hide her annoyance. Her voice grates Sylvana.

"Around. Where have you been?"

"Here. Waiting for you."

"Since last March?"

"Don't be ridiculous. For the past two weeks. Just as I always come here for you, Sylvana."

"How's Mortimer?"

"Don't bring him up, for god's sake."

Claire hates for Sylvana to mention her husband Mo, the semi-retired dentist now fishing on the stocked pond, even in the rain. Claire wants to pretend that she and Sylvana are the only two people in the entire universe.

"I just asked a question."

"Don't be mean, Sylvana."

"I'm not. Would you like some tea? It's just that I've been busy."

Sylvana is trying to soothe the younger woman. She wishes Claire did not have her hair cut so short, so bluntly. She wishes Claire were not so angular, so harsh; that she wasn't married to a semiretired dentist twenty years her senior; that she had an angry independence rather than an adolescent sarcasm. Sylvana knows she wishes too much for Claire and tries to refrain from it. Claire's whine interrupts.

"With who? Busy with who?"

"Bilma. Her and I have been cleaning this place."

"*She*. It is she and I."

Sylvana tilts her head at Claire. She wonders what makes Claire presumptuous enough to correct her grammar? It couldn't be money, though Claire was rich if viewed as an extension of Mortimer, which she was by virtually everyone except Sylvana. Is it because she fancies herself a writer, working on that stupid book, though she doesn't even scribble Sylvana a letter in nine months? Sylvana wants to know, but doesn't ask her questions. Once she had loved Claire, she was still sure of that. When Claire had told her about the lakes in Illinois and how the wheat grew right to the edges of them. What she wasn't sure of was why she still loved her, if she did.

They let their cups grow cold in silence, the silence easing out of its tension and becoming softer, even compassionate. They allow gazes into eyes, blue to brown, brown to blue. The silence traces their hands from ceramic to the vinyl of the placemats, and from there to flesh. Thumb on knuckle. Finger outlining vein.

*How could they have ever quarreled?*

It is the silence that asks this. They answer by gliding into Sylvana's bedroom and stripping the sheets before they ease into the bed. This is a dance they remember. The silence is playing their song. Sylvana sees a cool blue lake with stalks of wheat as straight and as golden as Claire's thighs. Her hands are a silent wind, searching. Maybe they could be in love again, instead of merely lovers. For an hour, neither woman can hear the rain.

Claire is talking about Mo while Sylvana is shaking a warm metallic feeling from her body. She must have dozed.

"What I need," Claire is always telling people what she needs, "is a financial base. I can't walk out on Mo without any money. You don't understand. You own all this land, this business. Money is independence. And what about Roger?"

Sylvana wants to scream, *fuck Roger,* but Claire hates profanity. Sylvana hates Roger. For her, he is a spoiled and immature *maricone.* He uses his homosexuality to manipulate his mother, who has never divulged her activities with Sylvana. The mother and son conspire to hide the truth from Mortimer, though Claire is supposedly writing a book about her adaptation to her son's sexuality. She wants to document her trials and therapies and is sure it will be a bestseller.

"Then I will leave Mo," she tells Sylvana, who is again asleep.

Bilma wakes Sylvana past noon to report on the leaks. "Nothing much, and the rain is stopping, too. You look tired."

"I am."

"Then why do you do such crazy things?"

Bilma hopes she sounds merely curious instead of annoyed. She tries not to watch Sylvana getting dressed, not to think how she became undressed.

"Who knows? But two in the same day is no good. Stupid. You know, I sit out at Blue Cypress Lake all summer and never give anyone else a thought—except the old woman, of course—and I'm back here acting twenty-three instead of sixty-three. Crazy, ain't it?"

On the porch, the two women reminisce about Bilma's husband, how he beat her, how Sylvana ran him off the property with a shovel, how the cops came and wanted to arrest Sylvana. Those were strange days, they agree. And they were long enough ago so that the women feel free to inflate the October afternoon with their laughter.

Until a paler female with plucked honey eyebrows and flawlessly shaved legs joins them. Claire. Then the three women speak about the weather, autumn storms and all that.

Mo approaches the porch, attracted by this subject like a hungry fish, as Geronimo is striding toward the house, sweaty and wet from the groves. He had thought to check on Sylvana, but he can't say that, so he pretends to think he has left his wallet inside. His new plan is to let everyone know—to let Claire know—that he spent last night with Sylvana.

"It ain't in there," Sylvana says. Geronimo is stunned by her conviction. He spins as if to leave, but suddenly understands that it would look like defeat, so he joins the weather conversation. He has seen a lot of weather, during the season and elsewhere.

Bilma sees the rainbows first, three perfect arches spread across the sky to the west. Each one has a complete spectrum, the blue visible against the background of clouds.

"Rare," they all agree, commenting on their favorite parts of the phenomenon.

"The way the rainbows are connected on the bottom, like they are holding hands." Claire clasps her own hands together in appreciation of her observation.

"That's not true." Sylvana is amazed at her own vehemence.

"Yeah, it is. They are connected. I mean, not like holding hands, but connected, yeah." Geronimo agrees with Claire.

"No. They are *not* connected."

Sylvana tries to look through the eyes of the old woman, to check her own perception. What she sees is that it is Claire and Geronimo who are connected, not the rainbows. She sees their hands joined solid as prisms. She shuts her eyes tight. Tighter.

"Well, maybe it's done with mirrors." Mortimer laughs alone and long.

In embarrassment, the miniature crowd disperses, leaving Sylvana and Bilma alone again.

"Stupid. Stupid, stupid." Sylvana repeats the word like an incantation.

"Who?" the-trying-to-be-merely-curious Bilma asks. But she cannot decipher Sylvana's mutter. Did she say *her and Mo?* or *Geronimo?* or something else? Bilma turns the syllables around in her mind, looking for an answer.

Over the next two weeks, Geronimo brings Sylvana *dulce de toronja,* a complicated desert of sugar and grapefruit pulp, which Claire eats, licking the tartness from her fingers and saving the sweetness on her tongue. Claire brings Sylvana fried fish from the pond, which Geronimo takes from the refrigerator and eats cold and greasy. Sylvana sleeps with Geronimo again and then with Claire, then with Claire again and then with Geronimo, and again and again. Her lovers are like a parquet floor and make a pattern she cannot see because she is too close.

Claire and Geronimo swell with the comfort of their routine, and neither notices Sylvana's new habit of averting or even closing her eyes.

It is the last day of the month that Sylvana again drives north to Sebastian. Only this time she is alone. This time it is during the day, and it is not raining. This time she is not going to a bar.

But to her lawyer. Francisco Alster, esq., does not make Sylvana wait very long. He is a prompt, efficient man with a passion for representing migrant farmworkers and suing the shit out of crewleaders and growers for decent wages and good housing. His small-but-steady practice of representing clients like Sylvana supports his passion.

Alster has always liked Sylvana, in spite of her chasing guys off her property with a shovel. He appreciates the way her hair seems to stretch and shimmer even when she is sitting perfectly still. He admires what he sees as her integrity, her self-sufficiency, although he thinks she is not always honest. But he is also unsettled by her. Perhaps he knows too much about her. Or perhaps he intuits that what she so easily inspires in others is not something she will allow herself to succumb to. Once he thought he might love her, but he thankfully talked himself out of it.

The years have made Alster cynical. He sees what Sylvana is doing as a selfish act, rather than one of generosity. Still, he cannot help admiring her. He has the papers ready per her instructions.

The secretary, dressed as some kind of court jester or a clown, comes in the lawyer's office along with the receptionist to witness Sylvana's signatures. The receptionist is dressed as an Indian and Sylvana is mildly offended, though she isn't sure why.

Sylvana writes out a check for Alster, shakes his hand, and suddenly kisses him on the cheek.

"How will I be able to contact you?"

"You won't." Sylvana smiles. The secretary and receptionist smile. Alster smiles. Sylvana leaves and they almost regret not asking her to stay for their Halloween party.

She drives west rather than south. Inland. Inland. She can hear the old woman's voice getting stronger and stronger. She can see the old woman sitting on the shore of Blue Cypress Lake drawing in the soil with a stick.

Claire and Geronimo circle the house searching for Sylvana. They spot each other and are relieved, but they think it is not like Sylvana to be gone alone all night, all day, a few days, a week.

Mo makes his annual plans to head further south, but Claire will not go. She cannot leave Indian River without knowing about Sylvana. Mortimer can and does.

The night Geronimo comes to Claire's lonely cabin it is cold. The predictions of frost have been borne out. Some of Geronimo's crew are tending smudge pots in the groves, lit to keep the citrus from freezing. He has brought her his favorite desert, *dulce de toronja*, thinking she will find it unique. He tells her how difficult it is to make, how one must constantly change the water while cooking the grapefruit pulp. Claire is enchanted by the sweetness, by the sweetness of a man who can cook something other than fried fish. Not all men are like Mo, she tells herself. Men can be gentle. Like Roger. Like Geronimo.

Claire's hair is too short and too bluntly cut, and it rebels against Geronimo's grasp.

"*Quiero templarte.*"

She does not understand his Spanish, but Claire likes the rugged sound of it almost as much as she likes the wide smooth spread of Geronimo's back. His muscles vibrate like animals caught in a brown velvet sack. Even in the dark, she can feel where the tropical sun has summoned his pigments to the surface of his flesh.

Bilma knows Claire and Geronimo are lovers before they do. She can't help but find the pair amusing, though as the new owner of the Trade Post Campground and Trade Post Fruit Company, Bilma has little time to engage in amusement. The season is in full swing. She vows to manage the place more aggressively than Sylvana did.

"To tell you the truth, the old woman let the place go downhill the past few years."

Bilma has no one to tell this to, so she says it to a small bird building a nest near the porch. The bird does not sing back to Bilma about the absence of hills in this wet land between river and ocean.

At Blue Cypress Lake, two old women squat and chant and braid each other's hair. They look into the sky and see the fine mist of rain which collects colors around the sun. They look at their shadows which form a single dark mountain on the sand. They look across the water for hours, for days, for seasons. And when they do not like what they see, they do not shut their eyes.

**Other titles from Firebrand Books include:**

*The Big Mama Stories* by Shay Youngblood/$8.95

*A Burst Of Light,* Essays by Audre Lorde/$7.95

*Diamonds Are A Dyke's Best Friend* by Yvonne Zipter/$9.95

*Dykes To Watch Out For,* Cartoons by Alison Bechdel/$6.95

*The Fires Of Bride,* A Novel by Ellen Galford/$8.95

*A Gathering Of Spirit,* A Collection by North American Indian Women edited by Beth Brant *(Degonwadonti)*/$9.95

*Getting Home Alive* by Aurora Levins Morales and Rosario Morales/$8.95

*Good Enough To Eat,* A Novel by Lesléa Newman/$8.95

*Humid Pitch,* Narrative Poetry by Cheryl Clarke/$8.95

*Jonestown & Other Madness,* Poetry by Pat Parker/$5.95

*The Land Of Look Behind,* Prose and Poetry by Michelle Cliff/$6.95

*A Letter To Harvey Milk,* Short Stories by Lesléa Newman/$8.95

*Letting In The Night,* A Novel by Joan Lindau/$8.95

*Living As A Lesbian,* Poetry by Cheryl Clarke/$6.95

*Making It,* A Woman's Guide to Sex in the Age of AIDS by Cindy Patton and Janis Kelly/$3.95

*Metamorphosis, Reflections On Recovery,* by Judith McDaniel/$7.95

*Mohawk Trail* by Beth Brant *(Degonwadonti)*/$6.95

*Moll Cutpurse,* A Novel by Ellen Galford/$7.95

*More Dykes To Watch Out For,* Cartoons by Alison Bechdel/$7.95

*The Monarchs Are Flying,* A Novel by Marion Foster/$8.95

*My Mama's Dead Squirrel,* Lesbian Essays on Southern Culture by Mab Segrest/$8.95

*The Other Sappho,* A Novel by Ellen Frye/$8.95

*Politics Of The Heart,* A Lesbian Parenting Anthology edited by Sandra Pollack and Jeanne Vaughn/$11.95

*Presenting. . .Sister NoBlues* by Hattie Gossett/$8.95

*A Restricted Country* by Joan Nestle/$8.95

*Sanctuary, A Journey* by Judith McDaniel/$7.95

*Sans Souci,* And Other Stories by Dionne Brand/$8.95

*Shoulders,* A Novel by Georgia Cotrell/$8.95

*The Sun Is Not Merciful,* Short Stories by Anna Lee Walters/$7.95

*Tender Warriors,* A Novel by Rachel Guido deVries/$7.95

*This Is About Incest* by Margaret Randall/$7.95

*The Threshing Floor,* Short Stories by Barbara Burford/$7.95

*Trash,* Stories by Dorothy Allison/$8.95

*The Women Who Hate Me,* Poetry by Dorothy Allison/$5.95

*Words To The Wise,* A Writer's Guide to Feminist and Lesbian Periodicals & Publishers by Andrea Fleck Clardy/$3.95

*Yours In Struggle,* Three Feminist Perspectives on Anti-Semitism and Racism by Elly Bulkin, Minnie Bruce Pratt, and Barbara Smith/$8.95

You can buy Firebrand titles at your bookstore, or order them directly from the publisher (141 The Commons, Ithaca, New York 14850, 607-272-0000).

Please include $1.75 shipping for the first book and $.50 for each additional book.

A free catalog is available on request.